HELP ME, JACQUES COUSTEAU

HELP ME, JACQUES COUSTEAU

GIL ADAMSON

ANANSI

House of Anansi Press Inc.
110 Spadina Avenue, Suite 801
Toronto, ON, M5V 2K4
Tel. 416-363-4343
Fax 416-363-1017
www.anansi.ca

Distributed in Canada by
HarperCollins Canada Ltd.
1995 Markham Road
Scarborough, ON, M1B 5M8
Toll free tel. 1-800-387-0117

House of Anansi Press is committed to protecting our natural environment.
As part of our efforts, this book is printed on paper that contains 100%
post-consumer recycled fibres, is acid-free, and is processed chlorine-free.

13 12 11 10 09   1 2 3 4 5

Library and Archives Canada Cataloguing in Publication

Adamson, Gil
Help me, Jacques Cousteau / Gil Adamson.

ISBN 978-0-88784-799-8

I. Title.

PS8551.D3256H44 2009   c813'.54   C2009-903513-8

Cover design: Ingrid Paulson
Text design and typesetting: Ingrid Paulson

*We acknowledge for their financial support of our publishing program the
Canada Council for the Arts, the Ontario Arts Council, and the Government of
Canada through the Book Publishing Industry Development Program (BPIDP).*

Printed and bound in Canada

CONTENTS

Heaven is a place where nothing ever happens.

TALKING HEADS

THE *LAKEMBA*

·· I SEE THE LONG, HEAVY SOFA
come skating across the linoleum and I step out of its
path. The sky outside the window is grey and most of
the people in the lounge are green. The sofa collides with
the wall, seems to consider the situation for a moment,
then heads out over the floor again. My mother looks up
from where she sits, her cheeks flaming red, a lamp tilt-
ing solicitously above her head.

She sees that I'm okay and goes back to her book: *The
Alexandria Quartet.* In her mind, a mighty library is
burning. Vellum pages float out the windows and are
carried on the breeze out to sea. My mother is in love
with Balthazar. The lamp swings to lean over the woman
next to her, as if to see what this one's reading. I see the

sofa coming again. A plastic duck on wheels drifts into its path and, with a muffled squeak, it is creamed against the wall.

We're on our way home from Australia on a boat called the *Lakemba*, and soon we will cross the equator. Sun glares on the wide deck. Wooden tanning chairs have been strapped down and the sea rises and sinks at an angle to the deck that is woozy. I sit on a plastic horse and lift my feet. I drift over the floor towards my mother. Her face comes up, flushed and young and voracious for Balthazar. "Oh Hazel, darling!" she says and extends a thin hand to me, but I drift away again, tables, chairs, other children, the eight-foot sofa, all moving in sluggish orbits.

"Are you hot? It's so hot," she says, blinking.

"Come back," she says, and we both wait for it to happen.

We've been told it can get a lot worse. But today is the fourth bad day, and anyway, I'm getting used to it. My mother's worried about me, not having any other kids to worry about yet. But I'm all right. All I dread is going to bed — the moonless night and the wild moving wall by my bed.

· · · . · · ·

It's night and we're eight days away from Vancouver, the ship still lost in the dark and nothing anywhere to show us that this is not a dream. Above the upper decks, festooned with small lights and nosing into the night, are masts and antennae and other strange lines and pipes and funnels. The lights chart the shape of the boat. The white floors of the decks appear to be an empty stage with spotlights shining down. The occasional woman totters by, the occasional boy in a wrinkled white uniform. At midnight, the captain marches past with a woman clinging to each arm. He walks a perfect line, as if magnetically attached to the pitching metal floor. My mother, unable to sleep, peers from the window of our cabin and sees the threesome pass by — a man with two female flags, waving in the night wind.

"There they are again, North!" she whispers to my father, who sleeps on. "How can they drink in this heat?" Then she comes and looks at me where I lie like a wiener in a bun, a rolled blanket on either side of the bunk and my body wedged between them.

Nighttime is a horror to me on this ship. I am so young I forget that every day ends with me going to bed. I sleep in the top bunk. The steel feet are riveted to the floor, but not securely enough, so with every lurch of the ship, my bed leaves the wall and yawns out into the dark room. I try, absurdly, to hold on to a flat wall with my damp fingers. The bed dangles on the precipice, decides not to topple over this time, and sails back with a sharp *whang* against the wall. This process is repeated, unrelenting, until I fall asleep. I think about our apartment in Sydney, the houses next door, the cardboard cluster of our neighbourhood, and in my dreams, the whole earth is swaying too, all the houses knocking heads and rattling like goods on a truck.

· · · . · · ·

In case we have to abandon ship, my mother has packed an emergency kit: Band-Aids, rubbing alcohol, scissors, stomach remedies, a small mouldy package of cookies, a knife, baby aspirin, a crossword book. We are heading for the equator in a headlong rush, as if to get the suspense over with and start roasting. The engines roar and throb through the metal framework of the ship. My mother, her forehead damp with sweat, is staring at the black heaving water, the deep valley and peak, and, close in the wake of the ship, the ornamental curl of white. She is standing on the deck at sunset, without a thought in her head, the emergency kit in her limp grasp, while behind her, through the open lounge door, come the sounds and moving shadows of a movie. People wander around the deck in silence and pass on down the metal stairwells. Someone is screaming with laughter somewhere, but, to my mother, it is the caw of a bird. The purser staggers by, his sleeves rolled up.

"Excuse me!" my mother starts, but the purser is gone into the bowl of the setting sun, a shadow-puppet jiggled before a roaring fire.

. . . . . .

My father has been teaching in Australia; an offer to teach one term in Canadian studies somehow stretched to two years. He's fought his way through the halls of a high school in Sydney, pulled maps down from the ceiling and poked holes in them with a pointer, read poetry out loud, sung with the woeful choir, and exchanged blistering wisecracks with other teachers. Not being one of them, he was looked upon as a kind of intelligent ape. After all, where he comes from, water circles the drain the wrong way.

My father has committed to memory folk songs, sayings, long heroic mining poems involving dogs and dynamite. He believes, privately, that marsupials are a perversion of nature. He listened to the red desert hulk of Ayers Rock hissing in the rain, an occurrence so rare that, when he told his colleagues about it, he was not believed. He ventured into the outback with bored guides and my mother swooning beside him in the Jeep; ate cooked snake; lay awake in the dark and heard the chuckle of night birds. He heard the low, creepy growl of the didgeridoo and the bird-like flutter of the bullroarer. He perfected his mimicry of the accent. He laughed out loud in restaurants and lunchrooms and barber shops and banks at things that no one else considered funny. He stood in the cool wind of Sydney Harbour with the gulls overhead and stared at the green streaks along the hull of the ship he must eventually board to return to Canada, and he wondered what else in his future could possibly equal this.

· · · . · · ·

We are passing over the equator. Heat stroke is epidemic on the ship. We are like John Glenn, burning through the atmosphere, falling to earth. The lights on the mast spark and flicker at night, rivets in the metal walls and flooring seem loose. No one moves on the decks anymore during the day. Cabin doors are left open, revealing the vague shapes of reclined figures within. Everywhere is the rising and subsiding buzz of the engines. The stairwells are clamorous, the lounge empty, and even the glorified mess hall unoccupied, except for a couple of drunken teens, and a dog lying flat under a table.

Earlier in this blazing cemetery, while Dad lay dreaming, my mother rose like a sodden ghost from the bed and staggered, furious, out of the cabin.

"Excuse me!" she said to the empty deck. "Somebody?"

According to my mother's telling of it, the captain was entertaining when she burst in. He had the two women there who had been engaged in a complex and private business with him since three days out. They all sat playing cards in their underclothes. My mother had her emergency kit with her, and she shook it menacingly at the captain.

"I've been to the purser, or bursar, or whatever you call the stupid man! And I've been to the engineer! They keep sending me to someone else."

"Madam—"

"I have children to look after!" she said, forgetting for the moment that she had only one child.

"Madam—" the captain said, rising and wiping his palm before offering it to my mother. She paid no attention to his hand or his grey underwear or the room she was in, but carried on as if run by batteries.

"I've tried to get that idiot man in E-12 to come out and help me. I have a child who's burning up. And now I'm forced to come here. This is the most shoddy, maddening ship I've ever been on!" She said this as if she had made a career of being on ships. The two women had disappeared into the murk of the huge apartment, perhaps into a closet or a bedroom or a toilet. They were just gone, as if vaporized. My mother blinked.

"Madam," tried the captain again, "how can I help you?"

My mother looked at him, her face slick with sweat. "If I don't get a fan in my cabin in four minutes I'm moving my mattress onto the deck!"

Now the fan rattles away, freshly bolted to the metal wall. I stand at my mother's side, blocking the breeze, and poke her in the ear. She brushes me away. I lean over and stare with one of my eyes into the dark brown pool of one of hers.

"You're sweaty," I say and she groans. She is lying on the unmade bed, one leg hanging off, when my father appears at the door with the doctor. As it turns out, my mother has dysentery and is running a temperature of 104.

"Oh," she says, "that's why I'm seeing those things," gesturing at nothing.

· · · . · · ·

It's Christmas dinner on the equator, and we're sliding down the leeward side in a luxuriant easing of heat. We're heading north, heading home, in a happy rocking nausea, and all day the smells issuing from the kitchen have been assailing my parents with memories. For my part, I have never seen snow. I learned to speak the language in Sydney, Australia. Now, inexplicably, all of my friends have developed Canadian accents. They say "Hi" instead of "G'day." My father asks me what I want for Christmas, which is strange, because it's not like he can go out and buy it. I ask for a beach ball.

In my future there is no beach ball. Instead, there is a plastic sheet that you use like a toboggan. And a torturous, unbending snowsuit — a whole world of children waddling around in torturous, unbending snowsuits. A world of sleds and snow and slush and ice-balls down the back of my neck and soggy knees and the maddening *zzt-zzt* of nylon snow pants; the throttle of wool scarves, yanked tight by my mother and impossible to claw open; the stink of cloakrooms; the multicoloured Popsicle look of cold feet and the shrieking pangs while they thaw; the blue-grey, motionless mornings when the backyard is erased by snow, the backyard where airborne debris lands, punctures the lunar surface, sinks out of sight. I will not get a beach ball.

· · · . · · ·

My mother is feeling better now, hiding in the cabin in case a bursar or purser should walk past, or in case the captain in his nocturnal wanderings should pass by with his women. But there is no one on the decks except the long, flat dog that slinks under tanning chairs and licks the painted metal floor for crumbs and spilled sweet drinks. I follow him and pat the stiff hair on his back and he ignores me. Together we cover the ship in a thorough and efficient manner, checking all corners and speeding past certain doorways where, perhaps, there is an angry kicked shoe or a flung book.

In this way I see people I have never seen before. Women with brown legs snapping their bathing suits beside the tiny, boxy swimming pool. Small men sweating in rooms that clang with pipes and meters and valves. Kitchen boys who steal above to stand on deck and let the cool air rush through their clothes, to smoke and talk together and flick the glowing butts out into the ocean.

I follow my dog until Mum arrives, furious with panic, having searched and searched and fled in her mind from the certainty that I had slipped under a guardrail and drowned. On wobbly legs she carries me down to dinner, where we sit with strangers, our waterglasses illustrating the concept of level, gravy searching the perimeter of our plates for a way out. Outside, the lifeboats rock in their steel hammocks, the canvas tarps that cover them undulating in the cooling breeze. The *Lakemba* chugs onwards into the sparkling Pacific.

Three years later, in the early hours of the morning, this ship will sink whole into the ocean, and these lifeboats will groan under the weight of panicking, sun-sick passengers. My mother will not be there to use her emergency kit containing scissors, cookies, baby aspirin. My father will be driving through the snow to work, singing out loud in his frost-dull car, perhaps wondering what the weather is like in Sydney, in the harbour, where the ships stand high in the water and the cranes swing all day and all night, carrying things away.

As for me, I will be enrolled in school and pondering daily a way to get sick or go truant or just get kicked out. A dog will be my only entertainment. I will be throwing biscuits out into the snow for the dog and locking him out and laughing when he comes back and hangs his head and drools the gummy pieces on the step, abusing me till I let him in again, wagging and snapping and soaking the floor with snow.

FEAR ITSELF

·· MY UNCLE CASTOR IS RICH.
He lives in a very large stone house that stands by itself
near the lake and is surrounded by tall spruce trees full of
crows. He has a fondness for animals, and over the years
he has acquired dogs, cats, pigeons, geese, a rabbit, and a
horse. All his animals are pure white. His main irritation
now is that he has acquired a second rabbit. He stands in
the middle of the lawn and looks at this new rabbit, points
at it and says, "What the *hell* am I supposed to do with
this?" It is mud brown. It is also a very happy rabbit, apparently, and it spreads out on the grass, with its hind legs
stretched back, and goes to sleep. My uncle storms away.

We have come to visit in the summer, bringing news
about other members of the family, fighting all the way
about whether Dad should turn the car around and avoid

this year's travesty. As usual, we arrive smiling, the adults tense and towering around me. I ignore them and run across an endless lawn, hop across the stony beach, and leap into the lake.

· · · . · · ·

Just after Aunt Netty left him, Castor had voiced his opinion that dogs are better than family. I think he meant that a dog will love you under any circumstances, no matter how much of a bastard you are. My uncle does not make it easy for anyone to love him. As children, Castor, my father, and the third brother, Bishop, were sent off to boarding school together. Once there, Castor was free to exercise his power; he was larger, more forceful than the other boys, and he had a knack for not getting caught. My father found cover in the library and studied geology, weather patterns, natural disasters. Bishop, armed with a mute hostility to everything expected of him, finally escaped Castor by joining the cadets and, later, the navy. In that school, at that age, my father says, Castor was fear itself. And now, alone in this house, with Netty gone, he's worse.

· · · . · · ·

There is a blow-up at night. I wake up to the sound of shouting and I blink at the dark light bulb on my ceiling. I can hear waves in the lake too and, closer to the house, something moving out on the lawn, perhaps a dog, nose down, hunting. I jump at the sound of a door slamming, and a moment later I hear my mother laughing. It's a laugh of exasperation.

In the morning, there is a game, to cheer everyone up. We stand on the concrete pier as Castor takes the cat, the dog, and the goose out in the rowboat. He tows the horse behind by a halter. The object of the game is to see which animal reaches land first. My mother makes vague objections, but she's just as curious as the rest of us. We watch as Castor lets all the animals go at once. Of course, it's the cat that wins, clinging to Castor at first, biting and scratching him until he is compelled to fling it violently into the water. Droop-eared and furious, it tries to get back into the boat until shoved away with an oar. All this time wasted on fighting the inevitable, and the cat still makes it back to shore first. It humps past us up the concrete steps, looking half its usual size, and streaks across the lawn to lie under a bush and hate us.

My mother takes me to the back of the house, where the garden is full-blown and wild and gone to seed. It has been that way since Netty left, "fed to the teeth with his nonsense," as my mother puts it. Still the roses and the vines seem to keep to the dark line of the soil, never crossing over to the lawn, and everywhere there is the hum of insects. We sit and eat lemon cake that my mother has baked. She sits cross-legged with me in silence. We put a piece of cake on the grass and watch as ants cover it. My mother and I share a fondness for watching insects from a safe distance.

· · · . · · ·

Days and nights drift into each other, punctuated by dinner, lunch, trips to town. Sometimes I hear fights at night, sometimes either my father or Castor roaring with laughter. One evening after dinner I get into my bathing suit and Castor and I go to the pool, which is big and concrete and shaped like an eight. There are leaves on the surface and the bottom is black with debris, but the water is clear enough. It is getting quite dark, so my uncle disappears into the pump room, and after a second the lights in the sides of the pool snap on. There is a loud hum. He comes out again, fighting his way through the bushes, cursing.

"Hope there isn't a short circuit," he says and I pause on the pulpy diving board and look at him. I back away, wondering out loud if we should poke the surface of the water with a stick or a rubber boot first.

"Only way to tell," my uncle says, smiling, "is to jump in." I realize I've made a crucial error by getting up on the board first, and start to quail. But Castor gives me that look, the black eyeball, and I run and jump, no hesitation. Up into the night air, then down and under the bright, glittering water, my arms ahead of me like a blind person. There's no shock, not that I can tell, so I open my eyes. I can see all the hairs on my arm. I watch them wave back and forth as the bulk of Castor hits the surface after me.

"You know what it's like?" my father says. "You go into your room and there are clothes on your bed from grade seven, laid out for you to put on. You're supposed to get into them and walk around like a fool." I frown at my father, waiting for him to explain what he means. He fiddles with his belt buckle.

"That's what it's like to come here," he says.

The two of them go out in the early morning, Dad and Uncle Castor. They walk into the woods with rifles. While they are gone, animals rush out from the trees, a skunk, a deer, the brown rabbit. They stop on the gravel driveway and pant. After a while they make their slow way back into the dark woods. Later my uncle emerges with my father following. They say they didn't find anything, that they just sat on a large rock and discussed my father's future. By the way my father is standing, the wild look in his eyes, I guess this is true. But later a neighbour comes round and says his dog was grazed by a bullet.

The neighbour is chased away by Castor, who follows him halfway down the lane. The rabbit hops slowly after them both, looking for attention.

My mother figures in all of this too, being under constant pressure to cook. Aunt Netty (whose name Castor will not allow spoken) is gone, so some woman must cook. My mother flatly refuses to cook for my uncle, and so we three sit down to a meal while he rages around the house, cursing. Once he points his rifle at me and threatens to shoot me. I keep my head down, keep eating. My mother acts like she doesn't even hear him, as if he doesn't exist. Eventually he gives up and makes himself some soup and comes to sit with us, slurping loudly, as if nothing has happened.

My mother pours me a bath. She says: "He just wants people to know he's alive, that's all."

"I know he's alive."

"Everyone's the same, Hazel. Everyone wants things to go their way."

She leaves me alone in the wide, cold bathroom, vines coming in the window, small black and white tiles on the floor, and steam coming up everywhere. I decide that I too want things to go my way, but I will never treat my children the way Castor treats my dad. I don't know it yet, but I have a little brother on the way, and despite my good intentions, I will torment him in my own way.

· · · . · · ·

One night, the adults turn the stereo on and let all the lights in the house burn. My mother and my father dance out on the grass in their bathing suits and Castor sits on the stone steps and watches, flicking pebbles at them. I am upstairs in the hallway, looking out a window, and I see Castor disappear into the dark, followed by a dog. When he's gone, my mother does a strange little dance, a belly dance, and my father leaps and twirls around. They are laughing, dancing to please each other. Then the huge shape of a white goose heaves past them, like a newspaper in the wind, followed by another and finally the dog and Castor. I stare down at the dancing flurry.

My mother is physically fantastic. She's long, tall, elastic. She can put her feet behind her neck. She can lie on her stomach, arch her back, and make a perfect U. Measured from fingertip to fingertip she must be six feet. Sometimes she would wrap her thighs about Dad and squeeze until he panicked and begged and struggled, like Faye Wray squished between the fingers of King Kong. When she cuddled him close to her and acted nice, he went almost crazy with desire. I suppose these are things a child shouldn't know. But I have my own unusual abilities, and can hear a conversation through three walls. After years of listening, I have formed an odd portrait of my parents.

· · · . · · ·

Two evenings later, I have my nightmare. I have been given some crème de menthe, which looks and smells like candy but burns like fire. I had whined for a glass until my father, who was getting drunk, gave me one. It was a calm, happy night and my uncle was pulling books from the shelves, excited, trying to prove some point. My father was saying "God, no!" and rubbing his face, but he looked sleepy and content, and Castor kept exclaiming, "This is it, North, this is what I mean!"

I sat and stared out the window at the lawn and drank my liquor. The grass outside looked like an empty stage. Castor was reading something out loud, intoning the Latin parts in a leisurely way, and my mother was twitching to get out of the room. In three sips, my drink was gone, and I went to bed pouty and uncomfortable.

"Think about nice things," my mother suggested. But I didn't. I thought about where my Aunt Netty was, lost maybe, out in the night.

In my dream the white horse gets loose from his stall and kicks at the barn door until it splinters and falls aside. He clops out onto the road and stands waiting, pale neck bowed. I hold my breath and watch helplessly as he lifts his head and sees me by the barn where I'm hiding. As he approaches, his eyes roll back and stare white at nothing. I wake with a jolt. And then I hear, in a far room, the sound of a man crying.

· · · . · · ·

My mother sits on the grass with her legs out in front of her and her elbows between them on the grass. She looks up from the paper.

"Seventeen people fell off a ferry into the freezing water near Baffin Island, and they all lived." My uncle notices the position she is in. He stares at her for a long time.

"That is *not* natural!" he bursts out finally.

My mother looks up. "Natural?" she says. "I'd call it good luck."

I wander behind the house and stand looking at the long, wilting flower beds in the garden, the brown leaves of the roses, the bald stems and heavy pink and yellow heads. The summer is getting on and I am trying not to think about school, which looms like a permanent seat at the dentist's. A bumblebee hums through the roses, struggling from head to head, then rises up and drags itself to the next bush. I notice another bumblebee to the left, and then another and then more. The wind dies down and, all at once, I can hear hundreds of bees. For a second I see everything alive and moving at once. I can't help liking moments like that. I had a teacher at school called Mrs. Vittie who liked to throw things when she got mad. She'd act patient for a while, then suddenly turn blood red, lose her cool, and throw something. One time she threw two chalk brushes, her shoes, books. Kids were shrieking and ducking. One moment the class was frozen, waiting for it to happen, and then everything started moving at once.

Today is the day before we leave Castor's and go home. My father has been in the basement rewiring the house. He tells me he can never relax in his brother's house and so he has to find things to do. It pleases him to change things, so switches in one place are attached to light bulbs in another. The pool lights are now connected to the kitchen. The hall light's in the one spare bedroom. As of last year, the bathroom light is somehow disconnected entirely, so we all have to go in the dark. I've never been scared in the dark because I can hear anything moving around, no matter how small it is. I know when I'm not alone. But my mother suffers. At night she will always take the dog. She calls it the outhouse, even though it's indoors.

My Uncle Castor is looking at us in a funny way. He has become sullen. I figure he is beginning to miss us, even though we haven't gone yet, and if you asked him, he'd probably say we were freeloaders, good riddance. He stands out by the barn and feeds the horse, brushes it and digs stones from its hooves. He takes the dog to the lake and washes it with baby shampoo and throws sticks into the lake for it. The dog crashes into the water until all the soap is off. Castor seems to be taking stock of his animals. The horse, dogs, cats, rabbits. The geese and pigeons he doesn't care about too much, but still he goes and looks at them, just looks. He bends over a goose, which stands on the lawn and goggles up at him. He shuffles his feet and the bird backs away. He stares at the spot where it has been.

· · · · · ·

The morning we're supposed to leave, I come down to the kitchen and look out the window that runs the length of the counter. It's a wet morning and mist pours out of the trees onto the gravel driveway. My stomach growls. After a minute I see my Aunt Netty standing at the edge of the woods with her hands on her hips. It's as if she's just stepped out of the trees, but most likely, she's walked up the long drive from the road. She looks at the house for a while, then walks briskly up the stone steps and through the door. A little later I hear Castor howling to my father, pounding on his bedroom door as if it is Christmas Day.

I search the fridge for something easy to eat, then I get excited about cooking something. Perhaps I can make breakfast for Netty and my parents. I have never seen any-one cook for Castor, and so the idea is alien to me. I take out the skillet and burn two eggs to black crusts before my mother comes rushing into the kitchen and takes the pan from me. Her long arms extend from the sleeves of her housecoat as if she has grown during the night.

"She came home," I say, and my mother laughs.

"She certainly did."

"Would you ever leave Dad?" I ask, wondering if this could happen to me, my mother walking off into the woods, or rowing over the lake.

"There are things that could make me; I won't lie to you about it. There's something about men and marriage that I don't like." She stood there for a second, thinking.

"No," she says and puts a plate of eggs down in front of me. "Your uncle and aunt are a whole different case. Don't judge the world based on them."

I hadn't expected all of that. I just want her to say "No."

· · · . · · ·

A spot of light falls through the tree above me and drifts over the plate of cookies, the silver teapot, and I watch it, waiting till the rest of the table is set and we can begin. We've decided to stay until evening. After all, this is his-toric; the first tea on the lawn since Netty has been gone. In some ways it seems she never left. Already there is a pile of brambles and dead branches at one end of the lawn, with several broken aluminum chairs tossed on top. Both bathrooms have been boiled and scrubbed, and the fridge stands open, defrosting.

Netty comes across the lawn with a plate, and Castor sits back, watching her come, and sighs. She's dressed in a long blue sari with gold paint on it. She wears bracelets thick as pipes, and her hair is turning white, much whiter than Castor's hair, as if she's been shocked by what she's seen of the world.

"Some day," she had whispered to me in the kitchen, "you may want to see the desert." I looked into her grey eyes. She smelled nice and her voice was soft and mesmerizing.

"In the Sahara," she said, "there are sandstorms so strong you can't breathe the air. And sometimes it rains so hard that many people drown."

"They drown in the desert?" I ask.

"Oh Hazel, imagine this for a moment. Imagine that you're sitting in a tea house, at dusk, and suddenly along come men on camels, dozens of them, beating the animals like this as they ride past you — *whoosh!*" She sweeps her hands past my face. "Terrifying." She grins widely.

I am in love with Netty. We all are, all of a sudden, in love with her.

And today is the day we have to go home.

· · · . · · ·

Nothing can stroll quite like a horse. Its white sides show through the bushes and then it steps out onto the grass, strolling to the lake. It dips its muzzle in the water and I follow, keeping a long leg's distance behind it, wondering how it has got loose. It drinks and shifts from hoof to hoof, stepping deeper into the water until it stands attached to its own reflection. I hear our car start up, then stall, then there is quiet again. The horse looks at me, a stream of water running off its chin, and I get a feeling I get sometimes. I wonder when we're all of us going to disappear, go our separate ways, lose everything.

Behind me comes a short laugh and footsteps. I turn to see my uncle come running, a wicked look on his face. The horse veers and dashes out of his way as Castor scoops me up into surprisingly strong arms and keeps on running, over the grass, me screaming, him laughing. And then the two of us shoot off the end of the dock and out over the water, our reflection like a spaceship falling to earth.

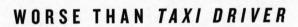

·· LIFE IS GOOD. I AM SITTING
in a dim movie theatre with my father, drinking flat pop
and eating licorice, and *Bambi* is about to come on. As
soon as the movie starts, I know my father will fall asleep.
The TV does the same thing to him; I think this is why he
volunteers to take me to movies: so he can sleep.

I ask him now, "Fold or rise?" and he says, "Fold." My father and I make bets on everything, and today it's whether
the red velvety curtain will be raised fold by fold or will
wheel itself into the ceiling. But I should know better. My
father has brought me here before and he remembers. I give
my father the thumbs up for winning as the curtain flops
and thumps its dusty way up and the short cartoons begin.

My exhausted mother is at home, lying across the
double bed as if she has fallen from a plane, and my new

little brother is asleep in the underwear drawer. My parents didn't buy a crib or changing table or anything until the baby was safely born, because my mother is from a Scottish background and is extremely superstitious. In her family, no one will leave shoes on tables, or go out a different door than the one they came in, or say anything optimistic without trying to find a piece of wood to knock on. My father's awkwardness and general optimism sometimes leave her stunned, considering the disasters she feels sure await them both.

And who knows, maybe she's right. Maybe the worst will happen, if you wait long enough.

But today she is asleep, one hand extended to the underwear drawer inside which squirms and kicks a new Andrew. My parents have been pouring as much attention on me as possible, ever since the neighbour lady gave me a doll. I thanked her nicely and went upstairs with my gift. I was found later shutting the bathroom door repeatedly on its head. My mother was very pregnant at the time. She and my father just looked at me. I pulled the doll's distorted head off and held it out to them.

The shorts are over and my father is already passed out, his hands on autopilot holding his drink and popcorn on his knees. I take a big slurp of pop and beam up at the screen. *Bambi*! Excellent!

But it's not excellent. Right away, Bambi's mother is shot dead by hunters. She murmurs a few survival tips to him, watches him play, and then *whammo*! She's gone. And as if that's not enough, the forest bursts into flame. It's the worst thing I've ever seen. I stare in disbelief at the screen, my mouth hanging open, my grip on the soft drink getting tighter and tighter.

My father told me later that he was dreaming about his brother Bishop. In this dream, Bishop stands on an ice field with the aurora borealis flicking on and off overhead like a bedroom light, and next to him is the mountainous flank of a killed whale. Bishop's mouth opens and a strange wailing comes out. It is a horrible noise, torturing my father's ears, and then it is joined by other voices, also wailing. In fact, most children in the theatre are in tears.

"Christ," my father says out loud, "why'd you bother killing it then?" At that moment, my grip causes my cup of 7-Up to cave in, and I geyser liquid over both of us. My father wakes up and staggers down the aisle with me weeping and hysterical, holding me out in front of him like a leaking bag of groceries.

· · · . · · ·

"Isn't he a doll?" the woman shrieks. "Isn't he an absolute doll?" She's brought jams and baby clothes and she's barely concealing her shock at finding the baby in the drawer. To cover up, she yells. Andrew has a towel under his head and he's wearing plastic diaper pants and he's looking up at the bristle brush of shapes leaning over him. I'm peering into the drawer as well, poking a finger at his feet. They look kind of comical to me, toes like corn niblets, and so does the way the baby seems to goggle at the world with his hair standing on end, as if he's never seen the like. His wide-eyed expression, we will discover later, comes from the fact that he badly needs glasses and can't see anything. He gawps at the shape of the lady and gives it a grin. She rings out like a doorbell about what an angel he is, and I have to leave the room.

· · · . · · ·

I whine constantly. It's been months since I felt anything but frustration. I stand in the kitchen and complain to my mother as she is making sandwiches. She says, "If you must whine, Hazel, go and do it on the porch."

I'm caught in a logical bind; I can't seem to stop whining, but she won't let me do it around her, so I give up and go out onto the porch. This display so impresses my mother's friends that they go home and try it on their kids.

Right now I'm as much fun as a rattlesnake. All my friends are away for the summer and I am alone on the street, with nothing to look forward to but the imminent arrival of my cousins. I have way too many cousins on my mother's side, none on my father's. This bunch all yell, their father never stops bellowing at them to shut up, and they travel in a station wagon.

It is clear to me that my life is both a misery and a bore, and for this I blame Andrew. He's one and a half years old now, and he's no fun at all. At the moment, he's only old enough to stagger around and pull things over onto himself; to shriek and then laugh at me when I jump; to throw things, with surprisingly good aim. Sometimes, I hand him a rock, then point him at other children, like a human slingshot.

I go back inside and sit and glare at my sandwich and grumble violence and death under my breath. My brother stares at me from his high chair. His hair is standing straight up and he holds a spoon, which he has a fondness for clacking against his plastic tray. He points the spoon at me and says something pointed and garbled.

"Holy mackinaw!" laughs my father. "He spoke French!" He looks at Mum. "We got a French baby by mistake." My mother and I scowl, unimpressed, while the baby blows spit over the table.

At this moment, the cousins arrive. The car door opens and the dog erupts from the car, then my cousins pour out like fish from a bucket. They thunder up the porch steps, one of my mother's many sisters laughing her head off. Andrew squeaks at the huge black shape approaching us all. I slip around the table and try to escape out the back door but am crushed beneath the paws of the Newfoundland dog named Brigus.

· · . · · ·

It's been a night. The adults all agree, it's been a night. The dark lawn still flickers with the shapes of children. My father has found some sparklers and a boomerang and a long piece of nautical rope. My aunt says, "Just don't hang anybody with it."

They've moved the kitchen table out onto the porch and lit candles. My brother is half asleep underneath it in a cardboard box; Mum has her bare feet inside the box, tapping her toe on the baby's backside to keep him quiet. She and I look out over the lawn, where someone tightrope-walks along the fence and the girls spell their names against the dark with sparklers.

My mother says, "Life is good when you're little." But the sister next to her snorts and reminds her of a few things. The two of them biting and punching and whacking with brooms, burying alive, hanging off banisters, jumping out of trees like Tarzan, fighting silently and in a conspiracy of nastiness. If an adult caught them, they would stand at attention, furious, with throbbing lip and grass in their hair. Fighting was private.

"Your body remembers fighting too," she said, and my mother nodded. Once a crazy old man had tried to kiss my mother on the street and she knocked him on his seat before she knew what she had done.

"I'm so sorry!" she said, helping him up. "But you shouldn't kiss strangers."

She looks at her sister now, who is pink in the cheeks with wine. Even I know that the two sisters are still competitive: who drives faster, whose memory is better, who saw a shooting star first. And the past is never forgotten. Last Christmas my aunt complained: "It wasn't fair. You were always Tarzan and I got stuck being the ape."

· · · . · · ·

Now I'm eight, lying in my room listening to someone's nose buzz in their sleep. It's another yearly visit from my cousins, and we have all chosen to sleep in my room, even five-year-old Andrew, who sleeps in my bed. His head points the other way and he's brought his hockey pillow with him. We're badly sunburnt, tired, and one of the cousins is allergic to something, her nose buzzing and clicking. Andrew sits up and his hand searches the bedside table for his glasses.

"Hey," he whispers, blinking at me through the lenses. "What?"

"Which would you rather eat, a dead squirrel or a live snake?"

Someone moans in his sleep. Someone else, closer to the door, says, "Dead squirrel."

"Okay, if you had to kill your best friend or your parents, which would it be?"

Two voices now: "Parents."

"Oh, nice."

"Okay," Andrew goes on, "what if you were..."

The voices blather on and I slump down in the bed, tune the sound out. You can get the feeling that your parents are the only thing between you and disaster. But I also know that people's parents do die. There was a girl at school.... I'm sure my mother could fend off just about anything, but sometimes I feel afraid for my dad — the way he drives, as if he's in a bobsled, whipping along, his elbow out the window. Once I had a dream that my father froze to death, his car broken down in winter on a lonely road. In the dream, no one would admit to me that he had ever existed. I woke up in anguish. That afternoon, he was pulling apart both the dishwasher and the lawn mower, and I didn't let him out of my sight. I told him jokes, asked him questions, followed him back and forth between the two mounds of wreckage.

I'm drifting off to sleep while Andrew and one of the cousins discuss the merits of using high voltage on the alligators who live in the sewers. No one has noticed the nose-buzzer, who has woken up and is now crawling silently across the floor towards my bed. In a moment, just as talk turns to giant spiders, her hand will seize my brother's leg though the covers and Andrew will go off like a train whistle, kicking me in the process.

Andrew's scream is legendary. He closes his eyes and his little fists shake, and when it's over he grins, his cheeks crimson. Everyone wants to hear it. The bigger kids at school, realizing that they get only grunts and complaints if they hassle him, have started paying to hear it. Andrew's been making some good money. In a moment, all of us, the cousins, the parents, the assorted dogs—perhaps even a few neighbours—will be rigid and wide-eyed, hearing a small boy falling from the sky, falling helpless through skyscrapers, dragging catastrophe down on us all. And then silence, followed by Andrew's low, kooky laugh and the weary thump of adult feet on the stairs. A house full of pounding hearts.

HEAVEN IS A PLACE

THAT STARTS WITH H

·· ABOUT NINE O'CLOCK MY
grandfather pulls up in his convertible and says do I
want to go to the beach. I think that's great and I run to
open the car door — but then I see it. He's got a dead dog
in the back seat, and when I say, "What's that?" he says
it's Rufus, but he doesn't turn around. "Aren't ya, boy?"
he asks, not looking at it. I'm just catching the stink when
grandfather gets an idea: "Race you!" he shouts, stomps
on the accelerator, and fishtails down the street.

My mother looks up as I scramble past her through
the kitchen. She can hear the sound of squealing tires
outside.

"Was that Gerald?" she calls as I hit the back porch.
"What's he doing?" But I don't answer; I'm planning my
perfect route to the beach.

When I get there I can see grandfather in his wide
trunks standing in the water, swishing drops into the air,
all stiff-legged as if this were the Arctic Ocean. Then he
makes a big whoop and throws himself in. The dog is
still in the back seat.

My grandfather is paddling around in the water. I go
running in with my clothes on to swim with him. It *is*
as cold as the Arctic Ocean. I have this urge to run out
again faster than I went in, but I just float there, freezing. Grandfather notices my face.

"What's the matter?"

"I'm fine," I say, gritting my teeth. When we get out
my grandfather tells me my lips are blue. This is a sign
my mother used to look for whenever we went swimming. If that happens, you're about to get hypothermia,
she'd say. The thing my mother finds so thrilling about
hypothermia is that you can still die even after they
warm you up. It's as if your brain stays cold and then
dies slowly while you sit there drinking cocoa.

We get back in the car and Grandfather drives me
towards home, but I tell him I want to go out for burgers, and he thinks that's great. He turns the engine off
and we glide by my house because my brother knows
the sound of the car and would come running out. Then
everybody would have to come and my grandfather might
be forced to do something about the dog. It is getting

late and the street lights are on, but the sun hasn't quite disappeared yet. It kind of shoots out at you between the houses.

· · · . · · ·

"What do you want on your burger?" Grandfather asks.

"Onions, relish, tomato, mustard, ketchup, lettuce, pickles, hot peppers, green peppers, mayonnaise, salt, and black pepper."

My grandfather turns to the little speaker outside the car window. "Every damned thing you got."

The speaker emits a crackle and a burst of gibberish and he says, "Right."

· · · . · · ·

"I do calisthenics every day," my grandfather says between bites. We're in an open field and Grandfather has parked the car facing upwind.

"I sit on my bum. But I'm not fat," I reply.

"You ought to exercise, Hazel, even at your age. It would build a good mind as well as a good body."

"Everything I eat has sugar in it."

"So?"

"So I might get overstimulated and have a cardiac."

"Really?"

"Really," I say and wipe my chin.

· 49 ·

"On top of that, Granddad, Andrew kicks me every chance he gets and I can't stay in one place that long. If I started doing sit-ups he'd be trying to sit on my face."

"Good point. You could always take up running."

"Flat feet."

"No!" he says, looking pleased, "You got that from your grandmother. At least you have something that makes you seem like family."

I sit and think about that for a second. "You mean I don't look like family?"

"Well," he says and looks down on me, "not that you look…well, you…frankly, no. I don't know where you came from."

"What! What do you mean?"

He smiles and bites at his double-decker burger. "Birth's a mystery," he shrugs. I realize he isn't going to say anything more. I feel like getting in the back with Rufus.

· · · . · · ·

My brother is clamped to the TV, both arms around it, his forehead pressed to the glass as he stares at *Rocketship Seven*. Commander Tom says, "Sit back, son, you'll ruin your eyes."

"No," my brother says in his little voice.

"Sit back, now. What if your mother walks in?"

"No," Andrew says and stares into Commander Tom's soul.

It is seven in the morning, a beautiful day, not a cloud in the sky, and I come down to find my grandmother sitting in our kitchen.

"I'm not going back until he gets rid of it," she says, embarrassing me with this honesty. I feel that children should never know about marital problems. Our lives are confusing enough.

"I'm not going back," she repeats.

"You want some Eggos, Grandmama?" I ask.

My brother shouts, "Me too!" from the other room, and his breath clouds Rocky the Squirrel for a second.

My grandmother is folding and refolding a napkin, and she says, "What is he doing with it, the smelly thing?"

"Maybe he misses it," I venture.

"Can't he miss something if it's in the ground instead of soaking into the Cadillac?" I know she's not asking me. She's sort of pretending he's there and she's talking to him.

I put a plate of waffles in front of my grandmother. "Blueberry," I say. "They're good."

She pokes at the crusted edges with a long, slender finger, scowls at the plate. The look on her face reminds me of how I felt when I smelled the dog, Rufus, as I was standing in the sun beside the car.

"That dog sure smells," I say.

"What dog?" Andrew calls. My grandmother covers her face and rushes from the room.

· · · . · · ·

"Andrew, let go of the TV," my mother says in passing.

"No," he says.

She keeps going and joins me in the kitchen. "What did your grandfather say to your grandmother? She's all upset."

"He didn't say anything."

"When was he here?"

"He wasn't. Mum...can I have—" But she has gone upstairs to tell my grandmother she's not fooling anyone, she's making things up; who in the world would keep a dead dog? I don't have a chance to ask her for money. I ask for money every morning, and if I get it I buy as much chocolate as I can. My brother takes his face away from the TV to glance at me, and his hair sticks to the screen with static.

"Andrew, let go of the TV."

He thumps his forehead back in place. "No."

· · · . · · ·

I'm in the backyard trying to do sit-ups. I get about three done before I feel my stomach start to rip open. I stand up and hold on to it. Andrew comes out back, his eyes like pinwheels.

"What're you doing?" he says, hoping I'll go back to it so he can kick me.

"My gut just ripped." I try not to move in case all the intestines come tumbling out. I imagine them looking like toothpaste when you spit it into the sink.

"Did Granddad make you do that? Commander Tom's a fascist. I ate Eggos for breakfast. Can you sing with your mouth closed? A is for apple."

"Andrew, go get Mum."

"This is a test; do not adjust your Indian. Have you seen the Breakaway Twins? Sound off at eleven," Andrew says as he goes back into the house.

"Hurry!" I yell and feel another little tear.

I know the truth then. Granddad's right. I am not really from this family. Something terrible happened at the hospital. Everything starts to make sense. I mean, at school they always forget who I am, and I've been there for four years! I could walk up to the teacher in health class and get weighed and she'd say, "Well, Freddie, or whoever you are, you've lost weight *and* a couple of inches! Do you eat properly?" I bet I could do someone else's tests for them and no one would know. And don't babies all look the same?

My mother comes down and sees me out on the grass.

"*I was the wrong baby, wasn't I?*" I yell.

"What in heaven's name have you been doing?" she sighs, and hustles me in to breakfast.

· · · . · · ·

"Where'd the dog go, Granddad?" I ask. Andrew is standing with me beside the car as grandfather roars the engine.

"What dog?" says Andrew, looking up at me.

"God! That smelly thing!" Grandfather bellows. "I looked around one day and couldn't believe it. He was *dead*!" He hit the steering wheel.

"What dog?" Andrew repeats.

"Is that boy all right?" Grandfather asks, looking closely at my brother.

"I have twelve teeth. Heaven is a place that starts with H," Andrew says.

"You know, young man, you're a little off-centre. You don't look much like your sister, either."

"Grandfather —" I want to stop him.

"Hospitals are terrible places, Andrew —"

"Grandfather!"

"— and I think you got packaged wrong."

"Prizes inside!" Andrew says, but he looks worried.

"Want to go for a burger, son?" Granddad says, and off they go, Andrew holding onto the dashboard with both hands, pressing his face to the glass.

BISHOP AND THE AUNTIES

is popular. Imagine a cold summer in Halifax, a restless-
ness in people, especially at night, and all summer an
arsonist is hard at work. Warehouses burn, ground-floor
shops roll smoke into the windows of apartments above,
houseboats flame out along the shoreline, drift away.
Finally, the Port Haven bird sanctuary down by the docks
goes up. On that night, when he's on leave from his troop-
ship, Bishop says, he follows the smell of smoke to the
huge glass dome, and he finds it lit from inside by flame.
The shadows of birds, wild for escape, batter the glass.
The uppermost leaves of indoor trees wave in the thick,
convecting air; glass overheats, bursts over the street; rag
bodies of tropical birds plummet through the night air,
lie struggling on the sidewalk, or pit the hoods of cars.

Andrew and I are paralyzed as Bishop tells it, his hands raised as if pointing out the horror. He lowers his voice and tells us the air smelled good.

"Malarkey," my mother tells us later. "He read that in one of those awful boys' books."

. . . .

On a mild Tuesday one midsummer, my uncle Bishop washed up on the riverbank near his home, barely alive. Perhaps it was a matter of drinking as much as he did, and then not remembering anything but shining stars, dogs as big as houses that passed by, growling at him, voices coming from far off, maybe the voices of the dead, and then fish. He was nudged headfirst into shore mud, burping and full of remorse, strings of snotty weeds and twine and rotten cloth draping his shoulders. It was a new story to tell his grandkids, he reasoned, assuming he ever got any, assuming he ever got married.

That's the problem, anyway. He's had women, one at a time, lined up over the years, and each one makes me and my brother call her "auntie." My father's pretty much had it with Bishop and his crazy women. With Bishop, he says, it just goes on and on. My mother doesn't mind one way or the other. She says Dad should be thankful he doesn't have any sisters.

All because of the most recent auntie, Bishop got drunk, got beat up, and floated down the river, so my father had to come and see if he was all right. The auntie left him, took almost everything he had, and said she didn't believe his stories anymore. That's the worst slap in the face to Bishop. His stories are his currency, his way in the world. It had never occurred to me or my brother that Bishop made things up. We didn't see how he could invent things like that. Andrew's always been a little scared of Bishop. Bishop the dog-shooter, the barroom-clearer; Bishop the noose expert. What my father says is, "If it isn't all true, it should be."

There's the tale about Bishop being in Brazil, going into a bar and seeing the courtyard decorated with a lost piece of NASA equipment that had blown off course and landed in the mountains. The bartender had taken the machine apart and pulled out the long sheet of paper with its squiggles and signs of the weather and the stars. He had strung it from the ceiling, like there was a party going on. Bishop says he called NASA collect, and the next evening men arrived in black suits, came through town like an invasion from Mars, and they got everything back, every last screw. The party was over. Bishop stood among the dripping trees, regretting his phone call, looking up at the stars and imagining a satellite burning to earth with its precious bell of information, needles in distress, recording every fiery moment.

You get to like him, my uncle, especially when you're little and you need a story to go to sleep. He's got a way of seeing the world, mostly as something that surrounds and centres on him. Bishop is in love with the possibilities of life. But eventually it gets to his girlfriends.

The evening of the Monday the last auntie left him, Bishop walked to town, following the railway tracks by the river. The pale river and the silver line of the railway pass together through the mountains here. Two lines tracing the dark valley, one straight and man-made, the other wild, uneven. And there, in the moonlight, was Bishop, walking along the rail like a kid on a wall, going to town, with firm plans to drink too much.

He doesn't remember exactly what happened, but, well after midnight, someone beat up my uncle and threw him in the river. My father assures us: he can be annoying. It was almost morning when he came to a stop, not more than a mile from home, floating face-up like a canoe, growling a church song through his swollen lips and paddling with the feeble hands of the near dead. Two boys ran down to the shore and put Bishop in their wheelbarrow. They took him to their house like a trophy, but their mother said he had to go to his own home, so they wheeled him back, following a line of trees, one boy under each handle. Bishop kicked at them and swore in all the languages he'd learned, and the boys grew frightened of his sputtering mouth and his muddy beard. They dumped him like a cord of wood in his yard and ran away home, the wheelbarrow jumping in the ruts.

· · · . · · ·

In Bombay, as a young man, Bishop had leaned from the kitchen porthole of a luxury liner, rested his tired arms on a load of soap, and listened to a strange, constant hum coming from the city. It intrigued him, this sound; it was not mechanical, not the wind, no kind of sound he'd heard before. And then his mind identified human voices, tens of thousands of human voices, coming across the water to him from markets and streets, spilling into the harbour. When Andrew and I look at a globe, privately we think of India as a noise. Those voices followed Bishop back to work and clamoured in his head as he napped in the early afternoon shade. Bishop asleep in Bombay Harbour. Bishop asleep in the mud of the riverbank, hearing the voices of two children.

It's way past midnight and I am supposed to be asleep. I *was* asleep, anyway, until I heard our car pull up outside. I know my dad is home. He's been visiting Bishop. My mother finds it unnerving, the way I can hear things through walls, doors, across great distances. Now I half doze and let the sounds of my father coming upstairs form themselves into an image of him, his coat over his shoulder, his shoulders bent. I hear my parents in their room, talking about Bishop, the aunties, a casserole, dogs, beer.

Bishop is becoming a story of his own:

I imagine it was dusk when Dad pulled up in his car, steam coming from the grill and a not-again look on his face. Bishop waved his hand hello, all jolly. He looked like the king of the mud clan, his fly undone. The two brothers sat in the light of a lamp by the kitchen, deeply breathing the cold air that flows off the mountains and picks up the scent of the river. They slouched down in their chairs, cradled beers, and closed their eyes, listening to an army of mosquitoes hum outside the screens. Once in a while there came the sound of an animal, something big, lapping at a puddle in the dark.

Bishop was talking about a woman, how she had winged a casserole at his head, and then earlier, long ago, how she had looked and what nice songs she sang when she thought no one could hear. He said she'd been a nun once and she sang in a choir with other nuns, and wore a grey habit, and she played the guitar badly. But she'd given all that up.

Still, she liked to get worked up on coffee and church singing; she attended surreptitiously, coming home like a tuning fork that won't stop ringing, passing through the rooms of the house one by one, as if looking for something. She had a trick she did with her shoulder—she could grind the joint so that it sounded like a galloping horse—which had used to make the other sisters shiver. She grew one white hair, only one, an event that Bishop found creepy. She wasn't scared of any of the usual things, like snakes or nuclear war, but she screamed if a light bulb blew out and left her in a dark room. She considered it a kind of ominous message.

This particular auntie claimed she had second sight, but it was a faculty she summoned only to accuse him of cheating on her. She believed she could tell the other girl's hair colour. In that regard, Bishop said, she was always wrong—but if you were listening to him, you never knew if that meant there was no girl or that there was a girl, but this auntie had got the hair colour wrong.

"Why don't clairvoyants ever use their power on the lotteries?" Bishop had asked her. "Why not do something useful?"

He also wanted to know why she no longer believed in his stories and yet, being an ex-nun, she believed "the most outrageous yarn in history," about how one young woman had managed to get herself pregnant. That's when she threw the casserole, according to Bishop, and my father had to suggest that Bishop had got what he deserved.

Bishop never cleans house, and so it was still there on the wall: a silhouette of a man in tomato sauce.

"Now I'm alone," Bishop said. "Single." And he scratched at his mud-hardened cheek.

· · · . · · ·

I am lying in my bed, in my room, but my mind is fabricating a strange, calm scene: my father and my uncle in shadow; time has gone by, I imagine, and tomorrow comes up silently like a bubble through water. Morning birds appear and scrounge around in the bushes, making the branches shake as if possessed. A finger of light advances along the river, stirring, stirring, digging up the clay shore.

"All these noisy birds," my father says, his head drooping. Bishop's voice is a hiss, as if he's never stopped talking, asking about my mother: Does she sing any songs? Does she ever throw things? He wants to know how early kids get up in the morning—what do you feed them? He doesn't wait for answers, but worries on about a life that is beyond him.

When the sun comes through the front door and falls across their legs, the two brothers sit up and hold their heads. Bishop staggers off into the bathroom and quickly falls asleep in the tub, where it is cool and the light is dim. My father looks up to see two identical boys staring in at him, filthy boys with green collars of dirt round their throats. His head feels like a wet cardboard box.

"Piss off!" he barks and the boys skitter off the porch and stand in the road. One of them starts to cry and then they go home. My father pictures Bishop in a wheelbarrow, limbs hanging over the sides like an octopus. Bishop with his scars, old and new, his fat lip, his choking snore from the bathtub.

Something about Bishop, something nice about him, is that he talks to dogs. Not just "Come here" and "Aren't you a good boy." More like, "Never trust a hammer, Toby, even if you wedged the head last week"; more like, "It's a sad world, Buster. Your friends should have told you so." And the dogs stare at him and angle their heads and whistle in their throats. Where Bishop lives there are dogs that don't belong to anyone — perhaps eight of them — big dogs that all look the same. It's as if they're a different species, my brother says, a race of giant dogs that only come out at night to trot along the riverbanks and snap at fireflies and dig holes in the clay and rip each other's sides open. They come and go like raccoons at night and Bishop feeds them, sits alone in the light of a lamp and tosses old bread to the dark shapes moving beyond where the light falls. He talks to them, shouts at them, croons to them about what smart, sleek, beautiful dogs they are. At night they jam their noses against his screen door and puff at him, or sit by the river and yip and howl, and the sound makes Bishop feel at home.

He's awake now, floating in the white of the bathtub.

"North," he calls to my father. "Are you up yet?" He thinks the tub around him resembles the never-ending morning of the Arctic, blue sun reflecting everywhere — you can't escape it. He's listened to the ice sing and mutter, the hiss of dry snow moving in the wind. He's shot huge, oily birds for food, shot caribou, shot dogs gone evil with hunger. His portrait has been printed in *Life* magazine: Bishop standing by a Quonset hut blown inside out by wind, his face obscured by scarves and beard and fur. The caption reads: *This man saved my life.* Bishop squirms in his bathtub and remembers the last auntie shouting, "It's all such crap!"

"Hey," he calls out to his brother. "You there?"

But my father is gone, having wiped strange paw prints from the hood of his car, slammed the door, and driven out to the highway. Mountains rise up on both sides of the road and in the car my father tries humming, which he always does when he has a headache. The air is light and cool and the tires flutter over the dry clay road. Dad slows when he goes over a bridge and sees the syrupy brown water where his brother passed like a snapped branch, singing and moaning and calling the last auntie by all her secret names. The names he whispered in her ear, and in the ear of the aunties before her, and in the ear of every small child falling asleep dreaming of the Arctic and the open sea and the many strange possibilities of life.

HELP ME,

JACQUES COUSTEAU

have gone out. Andrew runs to the window, then heads
out onto the street. He comes back in saying everybody
else has got lights in their houses. I check and see that our
upstairs lights are still on. So's the TV. Jacques Cousteau is
floating in the living room, staring out at me and my
brother, and here we are in the dark, staring back at him.
A huge black shark floats by. Dad crashes in the basement
and swears long and anatomically. There is silence and
then another crash. He's rewiring the house again.

This is the day I step on a live wire. I go down the
stairs ready to bother my dad, ask him riddles I've mem-
orized. I step down off the last wooden step onto the
concrete floor of the basement and next thing I know I'm
four feet ahead, still standing, and all my fillings hurt.

"Jesus!" Dad says, shaking his head. "That must have hurt." But I say no, and he relaxes, goes back to work. I don't realize how addled I am; I tell him my riddles, except I mix up the endings and they make no sense. Dad laughs after each one anyway.

He's digging in the fuse box, holding a mini-flashlight in his teeth. He garbles something to me and points at the workbench. I figure it's the screwdriver he wants because it seems to be sitting in the only clear spot on the bench. I go to get it for him, step on the live wire again, leap, then stand there watching the basement twinkle.

When I go back upstairs, Jacques Cousteau is hiding behind a rock. Andrew runs to the TV and turns the volume way up. We both like it that way. Jacques ducks as a dark shape glides by, and there are drums and tambourines and a screechy synthesizer somewhere under the water with him. I grab Andrew's cereal away from him, and he fusses and whines, tries to grab it back. We do this until we hear Mum pull up in the car. It's like the starting shot in a horse race. Andrew tries to hide his cereal bowl under the couch; I jump up, snap the TV off, run to the dark kitchen, look around at the wreckage I should have put in the sink long ago; Andrew skitters right by me and down the stairs to hide in the laundry room. I hear him hit the bottom step, and then Dad's voice: "Your sister did that too."

"That's it!" Mum is stamping across the floor. Between Andrew's panic about his cereal and me feeling guilty about the dishes I never do, I get ready for a gale force, but she's not mad at me.

"I've had it with Annette Batter, absolutely had it!" Mum's been visiting and she looks nice, a silky dress and ultra-high heels.

"Janey!" Dad calls from the basement. "I'm down here."

"If I hear one more thing out of her," Mum starts, clicking carefully down the stairs in her fancy shoes, "about that bloody fence, I'm going to strangle her. No, in fact, North, I'm going to strangle you." I run to the top of the stairs, watch her feet descend, getting closer to the bottom.

"Mum, don't!" I call. "Mum-Mum-Mum!" She steps down, the wire fitting perfectly into the finger's space under her high heel, and moves on, unscathed. She turns.

"What, dear?"

I stare at her. How does she do these things?

"What is it, dear?"

"I forgot to do the dishes."

"Do them now, then." Mum turns to Dad and says could he please, please, please be more careful when he parks the car, if he cares for her sanity.

My father drives his Plymouth Valiant like a crazy man: jackrabbit starts, corners taken at such a speed that groceries roll like waves across the back seat. The brakes are given a good workout and he parks in one move, palming the steering wheel and craning his neck to look out the back window. The parking space we have is exactly the size of our car, and every night he shaves a slice off the neighbour's fence. Every morning, when the car leaps from the gravel and bolts out into the lane, he shaves off another slice.

The woman next door dislikes us because our dog got her dog pregnant about forty-seven times, and also, she's mad about the fence. The thing she finds so maddening is that Dad never does any damage to his car. It's as if the Valiant is shaped perfectly to his task, the bumper poised, ready to peel her fence. Last year he tried to make up for it. He dug a new posthole and put in a new fence post, but she said it looked funny, stuck right out because it was new wood. He also sunk it right where the old one had been. The next morning, before he shot out into the laneway, he shaved a bit off that one too.

I run the water and start doing the dishes. It's quiet and I like the look of the soap bubbles in the dark. I splash around, flopping the soapy dishes up onto the drying rack. Both front and back doors are open and the dog comes clicking in the back door and heads for the front. Then he's gone again. Just as I'm finishing up I see a shape at the door, a small, bulky shape in a striped shirt.

"Why's it so dark?"

It's Taylor. He's five. Taylor looks like someone put Popeye in a saucepan and boiled him down. He spits with perfect aim. He gooses me once in a while, seeing as he's down there anyway, and I have always suppressed my shocked reaction, thinking that he can't possibly know what he's doing. After all, he's only five. But I've lately been wondering if that's wrong thinking.

"Where's the lights?" Taylor says again, and I tell him Dad's rewiring the house. He hears Mum's laugh and his body gets all jumpy like an eager dog's. Then he hears Andrew's voice and thumps across the floor, heads for the stairs.

"Taylor!" I shout.

Soon enough, there's Dad's voice: "Holy mackinaw! Did you see him jump?"

BIG BLUE SUIT

know for sure about my mother is that she loathes weddings. Take the one this morning. The limo is out of control on the snowy road, spinning round and round. We're all screaming. The trees outside stutter past and the clouds go with them.

We're ten minutes from the church, and the weather has made us late already. The limo is crammed: there's me, my brother, Aunt Netty, my mother, Auntie Odelia, and Mrs. Furstall, Odelia's mother, whom nobody likes. My mother has my fist in her hands and she holds it to her cheek in an iron grip. White balloons around our feet swirl and hip-hop up the window and hang there, suspended, until the car finally halts with a soft yank. The world is on a funny angle. My mother is rigid. Netty is trying not to fall over Odelia, who is by herself on the wide limo floor with her feet against the door. She is standing, effectively, on the door, hysterical, laughing and flapping her hands.

"Some driver you turned out to be," Mrs. Furstall says to the limo driver, who must be no older than seventeen. He's trying to scrabble his way out of the front seat, pushing upwards at the long driver's-side door. Mrs. Furstall, from her perch on top of the rest of us, swipes at his backside with her purse.

Odelia is another one of Bishop's women and, for some reason, she wants to marry him. That's why we're here with our elbows in each other's ears. We all slide out the door, careful not to come out in a slithering bunch, dropping one by one into the snow in our pumps and stockings and silky dresses, all covered over with our crappy everyday overcoats. The bride-to-be is holding her wedding dress up high, to keep it out of the snow, and you can clearly see her elaborate black panties through the tight white hose. The sight reminds me of someone's face crammed against a window. She stares down in horror at the place where her legs disappear into the snow.

"Mother!" she wails.

· · . · · ·

This isn't the only wedding we've attended lately. There was the one in the fall — me in my horrible pink dress, which barely fits me now I'm fifteen, and Andrew in his oversized powder-blue suit. Heather, a friend of my mother's, was getting married for the second time, this time to a Scottish guy with an accent so thick he must have stepped right off the hillside and onto a plane bound for Canada. The church was unheated, unadorned grey stone with a huge oak altar at the front and a life-sized oak cross beyond. It put you in mind of a cold-storage room. We huddled in the front pews and my father blew his nose and the honk echoed around the walls. Then bagpipes bawled in the hallway, making our hair stand on end. We couldn't understand a word of the service because the minister mumbled; the groom was paralyzed and had to be coaxed; the bride giggled her vows and pointed her toe behind her when kissed.

Finally, the bagpipes harried us all out of the church and into the autumn leaves, where we stood around under a lopsided tent, our noses running and our lips blue. The groom's father sat down with us and enthused incomprehensibly, his voice rumbling, his rough hands spread out on the table like two grey steaks. I thought my mother might enjoy herself, seeing as it was a Scottish wedding. On her side, our family is all Highland people. But she hated it, especially the kissing and the pointing toe.

"Heather used to be so forceful in school," my mother said. "What in the world happens to people?"

She says "people" but she means women. It's not the emotion of a wedding that bothers my mother, it's the ceremony itself, the sheer optimism of it, as if she's the only one who knows we're all on the *Titanic*. She's superstitious, secretly superstitious about everything. She thinks of luck as a malevolent, watchful thing, always present in your life. But it's not just bad luck that scares her — there's something else, something worse. In this way she is unlike any of her friends.

Gracey the librarian, for instance, is frustrated that none of her girls are old enough to get married. Angela and Gina are eight and twelve. But Gracey plans ahead; she already has a strong inclination towards blue for the bridesmaids.

"Blue's unusual, I know," she tells my mother over the phone, "but my Gina likes blue."

"Gina's a baby," says my mother. "She doesn't even have her period yet." Andrew, who has been listening, turns white and then red.

My mother is perplexed by people, disappointed by them. I try to figure her out, try hard to understand her. But at the heart of it, my mother is a mystery to me. And I believe, at the heart of it, she is a mystery to my father.

You can know basic things about my mother just by looking at her. Such as: she's big; she's tall and muscled and stately. Her feet are men's size ten, so she often can't find dress shoes in her size. She stands at parties in her stockings, a habit that gives people the false impression that she lives at the host's place. She is complimented on the furnishings or asked for directions to the bathroom. My mother makes an airy gesture and says, "Oh, over there."

Her legs are long and slim and seem to come straight out of the ground, out of her feet, and up until they get lost in her clothes. She has trouble finding shirts that fit her well.

"Pygmy clothes," she mutters, scowling at blouses in stores. "These wouldn't fit Andrew." This attitude may account for the giant size of Andrew's formal clothes, as if one suit should suffice until he's old enough to buy his own. The act of growing is something my mother estimates poorly, having herself grown far too big, too soon. She told me once that when she was a girl, she grew fifteen inches in one semester; she would sometimes yelp in class, clasping her arm or her thigh, which seemed to be tearing within itself.

Without heels, she is as tall as my father, which makes her six two. She hates rainy days because umbrellas come at her eyes with their tiny metal spikes. She bumps her head and her shins when sleepy, stands on bent objects to straighten them. She bends over the counter in the kitchen — cutting tomatoes, tearing lettuce — leans back and cracks her neck, sighs. One of her wishes is for my father to build a higher countertop; but when can he do that, he asks: *she* is always using the kitchen.

On the other hand, Dad will make all kinds of things for kids while they watch: Jacob's ladders, wooden swords and shields. There are kids up and down the street who own boomerangs my father has made from plywood, the angled surfaces carefully sanded and shaped.

Another thing I know about my mother is that she's strong. I hand her the jar of spaghetti sauce to open, and she pops it and hands it back. Baking a cake, she holds the bowl of batter in the crook of her arm and whips with a spoon, her arm flexed, never stopping or slowing or changing direction. Dad gets her to brace things while he hammers, hold ladders on which he teeters and reels, catch the ends of pine planks as they drop away from the screaming saw blade. She clamps her eyes shut and then, when her part is over, walks away rattling a finger in her ear.

My mother is practical, whereas I am not. Neither is my dad. He'll take two machines apart to fix them, then mix up the pieces. I'm even worse; I forget my wallet at home, go back to get it, and on the way leave my school books on the bus. Mum, on the other hand, can reach into her bag and bring out anything she needs: tape, a screwdriver, a spoon, notepaper, scissors, coffee, sugar packets, an eraser, elastic bands. She uses the screwdriver to jimmy the back door because Dad always locks her out. She uses the notepaper to abuse him about it, taping snarky messages to his windshield.

She has a voice that is so like the one inside my own head, I can never remember its exact sound. She and Dad take turns reading books to Andrew at bedtime, as they did to me when I was young. At night, I listen to her spreading the story out, soothing Andrew to sleep, her own existence disappearing into the many forests and riverbeds and snow-covered plains, the hovels and caves, the bad sisters, the evil witches, and the beautiful men. She sits upright on a chair beside Andrew's bed, leaning towards the light, unimpressed by what she reads, privately extracting from each story the dynamics between men and women, the perverse lessons being delivered, the critical warnings that are withheld.

She tells my father that "The Little Mermaid" is an evil pile of nonsense, and "The Ugly Duckling" is for saps. It's mean, she says, to suggest to ugly little kids that some-day they'll walk into a room and all heads will turn and they'll instantly get dates and end up on TV. My mother says we all have to face facts, eventually.

My mother is the only one who slams doors in our house. It's not an angry gesture, though, it's just her excess energy. She whangs the car door shut, deafening the rest of us. She elbows the fridge door shut, and jars within rattle in muffled complaint. She walks out the front door and pulls it shut behind her and the frame lets go a few more slivers. The slivers fall down through the air and land on little piles of other slivers; this is how archaeology happens: layer after layer of what happens, falling down and, after a time, covering each other up. Facts, hidden away.

Like the fact that she left us when I was very little. No one has told me, but I know something about that, having heard halting references to it through walls and doors, the silent challenge of man to woman, or woman to man, the strange unequal dialogue between unequal people. I know that she was gone for a week. I know that she took the white car. I know she came back, missing her husband, lost without her baby, came back in a different car, not the white one anymore, but our green Valiant.

I look in the photo album, at the one picture of a white car, just the back end of it in the frame, a dog looking at the camera and my grandfather laughing, and my mother's long, tanned arm reaching in from nowhere, reaching for the dog. I look at that photo the same way people look at the lines on their palms, trying to analyze the signature hidden there.

Bad luck hides in your life, masquerading as something simple, something pleasant. I learned this from my mother.

This winter there've been a ton of bad-luck winter weddings, the cold seeping into churches through coloured glass and loose doors, people hustling through the vows. My mother has been in agony, and Andrew and I haven't been happy either, what with the dreadful clothes, worn and dry-cleaned and worn again. My mother made my father promise: no more commitments. But then there was the girl down the street who was visibly pregnant. We had to go to that wedding or people might think we were stuck-up. At the reception, the bride's father and the groom's brother got into a slug-fest that rocked two tables, crossed the dance floor, and spilled out into the hotel lobby, where it was stopped dead by a large door-man in a top hat. After that one, my mother said she had trouble relaxing. She took all the iron heating grates out of the walls and scrubbed them until the paint was thin.

My mother tries to be rational and logical, tries not to let us see the many times she leans over and surreptitiously touches wood.

"Superstition is a terrible thing," she says, "and I'm glad I haven't infected you kids with it." But Andrew thinks stepping on a crack will break his mother's back — just like all little kids. He also believes that a hat on a bed will get someone killed.

"Where did he get that?" I ask her.

"Not from me," my mother says, sounding unsure. As for me, I believe all bad luck comes in threes, except for the kind that comes in fours.

· · · · · · ·

One night not long ago, Andrew dreamed that grandfather died at sea, drowned in the thick, black waves, and he woke up shouting for someone to help.

"Don't worry," my father said, holding and rocking him. "Your grandfather would never die; he's too much of a bast—"

"North!" my mother said.

"Well, it's true! He's stubborn. And anyway, he floats. All old men do." The next day, Mum worried about grandfather, as if my dad's flippant talk would bring on some kind of disaster.

"Think how we'd feel if something *did* happen to him," she said.

"Sure," my father replied. "I'd feel terrible."

The next day was my fifteenth birthday and we were out in the backyard with paper hats on. There were streamers strung along the fence, snarling together in the breeze, and a howl of tires as my grandfather arrived to celebrate. He had·a long scrape down one side of his Cadillac. There was also a bag full of my granny's dresses in the back seat, which he pushed me into trying on, one after the other. His birthday gift to me.

"There!" he bellowed, as I stood before him in polyester paisley. "Doesn't she look fine in that?" I gazed down at an unravelling hem whiffling in the breeze. When I looked up again, I saw my mother, her eyes locked on my father. She'd decided he was to blame for this, but she hadn't figured out how, exactly. And just then, Andrew came crashing out of the house, skipped down the steps, and hugged grandfather's leg.

My father is aware of his place in this system of trouble. For one thing, there's his family—that alone would do it. Then there's his ability to sleep through anything: movies, bad parties, weddings. Then there are all the little mistakes he has made, such as the time he washed his gardening shoes in the kitchen sink, the smell of dinner combining with the odour of warm fertilizer. He looked up, the shoe suspended over the drain, and noticed my mother's horrified expression.

"What?" he said furiously, trying to bluff her out. "Do you want me to track this stuff through the house?"

Sometimes I agree with him, or perhaps I just decided to agree with his side of the fuming dialogue of body language. My parents refuse to fight in front of Andrew and me. They think this makes things better. But in the end, it's just the same.

Sometimes I feel sorry for my mother.

"I could call Connie," she will say, looking at the phone. "It's been ages since I called Mother."

But in Mum's family you don't spend money on phone calls; you save it up and come for a visit. That's why we never see her parents. To my mother's mother, long distance means one thing: someone died. On the other hand, you never know when my father's family might come walking up the drive: no gift, no warning, no particular plans to leave. Sometimes we have come home to find a relative in the bath or my grandfather rifling through my parents' drawers.

Mum said that when she was little, growing up on the prairies, she would walk out into the field and not stop until she knew she was too small to be seen. "The thing I liked most in the world," she told me, "was to just be quiet somewhere, in a field or under some trees, and no one in the world knew where I was."

. . . .

I think about my mother, stuck here with all of us, all our stories and fibs and downright lies, our troubled course through life. And today, Uncle Bishop is getting married for no reason. Bishop and his new woman, Auntie Odelia, hysterical and up to her shins in snow; a limo in a ditch; my poor mother in shock.

We hurry along the winding road in the snow, looking like an assortment of bonbons in frilly wrappings, Andrew tugging at his too-big light blue suit, like a boy in a bag. My father and I cornered him after breakfast and wrestled him into his pants while he wailed. Once they were on him, he was like a broken horse, allowing us to slip the jacket on, do up the top collar button, tighten the little tie. He stood there in the hall, trussed up and glaring.

Inside the church, we look for a place to hang our coats and, right away, I see what seems to be a little closet against the wall.

"There, look!" I say and am well on my way before my father snaps me back by the upper arm.

"That's a *confessional*," he whispers.

The wedding proceeds in a kind of fluttering rush from badly played organ music to the wobbly-kneed bride fainting and eventually finishing her vows from the floor. The bridal corsage explodes in the icy wind, leaving nothing but stems tossed backwards over the bride's shoulder, and directly into the eye of Mrs. Furstall, on whom, my grandfather says, the promise of being the next to be married was clearly wasted. On we go in a giddy race until it is mercifully over, people driving into the darkness towards home, loosening ties, kicking off shoes.

My mother sits upright behind the wheel, her eyes wide and white in the rear-view. My father sleeps, just as

GIL ADAMSON

he slept through the service, the alcoholic reception, the shrill dispute between grandfather and Odelia, the bride's storming out, and Mrs. Furstall's final, acid summation of our family character. We drive, the headlights tracing wearily through the dark, and when we pull up behind the house, my mother sits with her head back on the wide bench seat and the overhead light beaming weakly on her face. We leave her to whatever thoughts she might have, uneasy in our own hearts and wanting to get away. Dad carries Andrew into the house, the boy fast asleep and slithery in his loose suit like a fish in plastic, only to find Bishop, the groom on his wedding day, passed out in his tux on our couch.

I see my father's expression before I see Bishop. I imagine it to be the expression people have on their faces the split-second before a car wreck. At that moment, I see the future clearly, recognize the shape of it, the wild and treacherous promise, the way it has always been nearby, waiting.

BIGFOOT

.... MY GRANDFATHER IS STAND-
ing in his housecoat, which he calls his smoking jacket.
It's got guns and dogs and panicking pheasants all over
it. On the table in front of us are burnt hamburgers, burnt
buns; somehow I even let the pickles dry into little green
tongues. My grandmother reminds him, "Hazel made
dinner. Sit down and eat. What's the problem?" But he
doesn't move.

"Well, yes —" Grandfather starts.

"Sit down," Grandmother says again.

"Do you know that I've eaten mastodon?" my grandfather says, shifting from foot to foot. We've all heard this
story before, and we ignore him, fiddle with our burgers,
discover that the buns are really quite edible on their own.
Grandfather sits down.

"Do you know what a mastodon is, Andrew?" he asks, and Andrew stares at him with obvious fatigue.

"He's making this up," my grandmother says. "There never was any mastodon."

She is sitting back, her hands in her lap, staring at her plate. Her hair is white-blond, like corn silk, and swept back off her forehead. Her eyes are very blue.

My brother and I have heard this story before, and we've heard our grandmother's versions, which are numerous and have nothing in common except that they are the negatives of his. That's what their relationship is like; whatever he says, she says it isn't true, even on the occasions that it might be true.

Since our parents left, on a long drive to sort things out, I sleep in Andrew's room laid out on the floor on an air mattress. Andrew claims that I shout and laugh in my sleep. From the look of him in the mornings, maybe I do. My grandfather is sleeping in my room and my grandmother is in our parents' room. They creak back and forth during the night, visiting each other, whispering. I sit up late, reading poetry and scrawling in my notebooks, and I can see my grandfather's shadow move across the crack under the door. The floorboards bend under his weight. I can't see him, but I know he's wearing Dad's blue dressing gown, the one with teeth marks at the hem from the dog. My grandparents don't know it, but I can hear what they're saying; they are discussing my parents. After a while, I plug my ears.

· · · · · ·

According to family history, my grandparents spent their honeymoon in Russia during the first five-year plan. Granny says that at midday on the day they arrived, the Moscow sun was weak and bluish, and the air smelled dull, like hot metal. She pronounced the food delicious and gained twelve pounds, but my grandfather poked at things, left his plate full. In one restaurant, he complained about the price for fish and, to his shock, everyone in the place shouted at him at once, including the cook. He claims that, at plays, Russians applaud in unison. At intermission they walk in circles, in a clockwise direction. Outside, there is no discernible division between a sidewalk and the street. The Russians, he decided, are big on togetherness.

Nineteen-thirty-something. That's when the mastodon was found, emerging whole from a glacial wall, preserved and impossibly huge. And before the scientists could get there, relics were taken, steaks cut, hide removed, the waist-thick tusk sawn off as close to the ice as possible. I imagine the mastodon entering the air shoulder first from a glacier, eyes cloudy, and people standing around, examining the dubious shape, the drip and stream of melting matter. I imagine the smell.

But it's all crap, really. These days, I don't believe my grandfather any more than his wife does.

And that's what bothers me: why don't I? It's not like I'm above believing stuff like that. As a teller of tall tales, my uncle Bishop is far worse. Even my father, on the odd occasion, throws fact to the wind and makes things up.

As for me, I have to stay away from grocery store tabloids because their crazy ideas stick with me. I remember them in detail: Elvis, JFK, Jackie Onassis, walking trees, bloodbaths, Satan, impossible babies. It's hard to fight the desire for it all to be true. I watch movies made especially for fools like me, my mouth hanging open: *The Exorcist, Rosemary's Baby*. They enter my dreams, woven together into a surreal combination, and I wake with a desire to check myself for marks and signs. Good Kirk fights bad Kirk in the vestibule of time. Body snatchers grow in the pumpkin patch. HAL the computer can lip-read.

And yet my grandfather can tell me he swam in the lake last night, and I won't believe him.

I force Andrew to stay up at night, shining the light in his face to keep him talking. My brother accepts the family history according to Grandfather, the picture of us that he creates, the things he insists are true and solid and real. To Andrew, questioning this is like wondering if the dog bites. Sure he does.

· · · . · · ·

One evening, my dad calls from somewhere up north and his voice is thin and strung out. My mother is in a coffee shop across the highway, he says, so we speak only to him. I can hear trucks going by in the background. My grandmother takes the phone. I hear Dad's voice like a mosquito, but I can understand every word. Dad calls his mother "Mother" and his father "Father." He thanks them for looking after Andrew and me and asks if we're behaving. When it is over, Andrew goes up to his room and closes the door and stares unseeing at a comic. I go outside.

For the next few nights I dream about trucks, about driving a huge truck into the dark, the steering wheel going crazy in my hands, the vehicle skidding and barely missing trees. Andrew and I both wake up the same way every morning: it takes a moment or two, but then we realize we're still stuck with our lives.

To keep busy, my grandmother is trying to teach me a few useful things, such as how to cook and use a sewing machine. Last summer it was knitting, which is one of the few things she doesn't do very well. I took to it like it was illicit and knitted everybody something absurd for

Christmas. My mother got a tank top made of butcher's string. My best friend, Jeannie, got a pair of wool boxers with tinsel and chestnuts worked into the pattern. Jeannie put them up on her wall and her mother told her I was crazy.

This anarchy wasn't what my grandmother had in mind. So she is trying now with sewing. But I snarl the thread into pom-poms and run the needle through the edge of my finger. Predictably, my performance in the kitchen is no better.

My grandfather reads the paper and complains that Andrew isn't small enough to sit on his knee anymore. He acts as if Andrew grew on purpose. Once in a while, he goads my brother into trying again and then makes a big deal about how his leg almost broke from the weight.

Before my grandparents arrived, I collected all my poems and notebooks and old childhood drawings of other planets and I hid them behind the furnace. I thought I was safe from his teasing then. But, the first morning, Grandfather came down holding one of my earrings he'd found on my dresser — a silver fish skeleton. He promised to find a dead cat for me to wear around my neck. The earring is gone, perhaps dropped by him in a garbage bag: ten bucks down the drain. It bugs me sometimes when I consider the appalling things he wears.

Now Andrew is outside with a bunch of other little boys. They are popping the top off a yogurt cup by combining baking soda and vinegar. This is explosion number five. The littlest boy is standing with one sandal on the lid and they are all shrieking with excitement. I can hear my grandmother in the kitchen, going through the cupboards, irritated about something. It is a warm, airless day. Cloud has settled low in the sky. There are puddles forming in the narrow alleyways between houses, spiders string their webs everywhere, and the branches of the highest trees look rotten and wet.

My grandmother is planning to teach me to bake a cake this afternoon, lemon cake, my favourite. But today I can't stand any more lessons. I just want to be alone. A series of images flies through my mind. A roast chicken, white as my underarm, hard as a rock, with stuffing extruding out its rear end like wet sand; a Jell-O mould with sockets where the cherries slid out; a cream of mushroom soup that smelled like an ashtray left out in the rain. I'm not sure I can stand another moment of it, my grandmother's smooth, graceful hands taking the bowl away from me, whipping the batter with stunning speed and, despite her efforts, the cake coming out stunted and gooey, with my name written all over it.

And then it hits me: no cake today. Andrew has exploded all the baking soda. I see the yogurt cup spurting and hissing like a sick toad on the sidewalk and little boys screaming, kicking it. My grandmother comes thumping across the carpet to see what the noise is and so I hit the road out the back door. All I want is to lie in the back seat of my grandparents' Cadillac and read poems or watch the clouds sink lower and lower.

· · · . · · ·

Like so many of the other things he sorts and compares and commits to memory, my father has a fondness for weather. He collects magazine pictures of tidal waves and tornadoes and sheet lightning. He has photos of storm fronts on the prairies moving towards the camera like grey walls. He has photos of clouds forming over mountains, slide after slide of cirrus, nimbus, cumulus. Clouds that resemble the sand in shallow water or the waves in a girl's hair. Clouds that bulge like muscle, or streak and ribbon.

In his classroom at Willow Heights High School, there are aerial shots of Mount St. Helen's exploding, diagrams of the directional forces inside twisters, a map showing the incidence of human deaths caused by lightning. Rangers get hit a lot. They hold up blasted hats as proof for photographers, complain of bald spots, ringing ears, a leg that won't stop trembling. Women almost never get hit because, unlike men, they opt not to adjust the TV aerial in a storm. Dad says you can feel lightning coming, a tingle in your feet and calves, a searing in your mouth. If this happens, he says, throw yourself down and roll on the ground. Lightning comes from two directions, the ground and the sky.

"Like any current," he says, "two sides must connect or nothing happens."

I remember him running his fingertip along a flickering fluorescent tube at school, the blue flashes following his finger to the other end and the tube snapping on. I remember him counting between the lightning and the thunder, saying every fourteen beats is one mile. Or maybe he said every beat is fourteen miles? I can't remember. And now he's not here to ask.

I lie in the car and look up and hear a thin rumble come across the sky, without a flicker of light from anywhere. I put the convertible top up and listen for the sound of rain on the tattered black canvas.

I'm feeling bad about Andrew. I should be helping him, but I can't even help myself. Last night, he wanted to know if I thought Dad and Mum were going to split up, and I told him to shut up. It popped out so fast and mean that I surprised myself; I couldn't even say sorry. He was quiet for a long time, holding on to his covers. And then he said, "Where's the coffee shop?"

"What?"

"Where Mum was."

"Who knows, Andrew? Who cares?"

It's funny how your mind works. Someone says don't think about dogs and suddenly your mind is filled with dogs. I knew where my mother was. I could see it. The walls were white, the tables brown, she was smoking and there was a man coming along the row of tables with a pot of oily coffee. There were trucks parked outside and people leaning on cars, filling their tanks at the pumps. My mother was watching my father's shape in the phone booth, and he was looking back at her shape in the window of the café.

How stupid can I be? I get fooled all the time. I believe Bigfoot exists, I really do. But such things are easy to imagine because they don't have to be true; it isn't important. I feel bad about my brother, because he wants some impossible things to be true.

It's getting dark out, and the lights from the house illuminate the inside of the convertible roof. Rain pelts down on the car and things feel different, as if I might have fallen asleep without noticing. Gradually, it comes to me that I have been asleep with my book lying open on my stomach. There is a radio playing somewhere nearby and so I sit up to see what is going on.

"Oh, Jesus God!" My grandfather twists himself round in the front seat. "Where did you come from?" The baseball game is on and he's sitting there in his white undershirt and bathing trunks. He's soaked with rain and he looks happy—or he *would* look happy if he wasn't holding his chest against a heart attack.

"I've been asleep, Grandfather," I croak, quickly sitting on the poetry book.

"What have you got there?" he snaps right away. Reluctantly, I hand e.e. cummings over to him. He opens it and stares, then reads out loud.

"'i sing of Olaf glad and big / whose warmest heart recoiled at war: / a conscientious object-or'...What is that? I don't think that's poetry. Object-*or*?"

"Grandfather..." I try to take the book back, but he holds it out of my reach.

"...'to eat flowers and not to be afraid?' Oh boy."

He hugs the book close and keeps reading. Rain pelts the car and I watch it drool off the tops of the windows and confuse the image of our back fence. I'm getting used to ridicule. Kids at school make fun of everything everybody does. Reading poetry isn't so bad; at least I don't have huge boobs, or flood pants, or a case of acne. I'm not in the chess club. I don't have a name like Bogdana or Flower. Things could be worse.

"That one's not bad," Grandfather says, poking a page, and then he gives the book back to me and sits still for a moment, holding the wheel. He taps at the glass over the red brake indicator. "Do you know that I used to write poetry?"

"Before or after you ate mastodon?"

"Never mind, then." He snaps his waistband, annoyed.

"Granny told me," I concede.

"Huh...well," he says.

Actually, Granny had showed me some of his poetry, and it wasn't embarrassing; in fact, some of it didn't rhyme. From the looks of it, he'd written a ton. The poems were all dedicated to her, and not one was about love. Grandfather shifts in his seat a little, then turns the radio up louder and we listen to the Blue Jays and the Angels get rained out.

When we come in for dinner, Andrew is in the kitchen alone. He is standing on a chair stirring a pot of soup. The kitchen is dark. Grandfather and I stand in the hall and watch the shape of my brother cooking in the diminishing glow of the burner under the soup pot.

"We blew a fuse," Andrew says without looking up. Then the lights come back on and we can see that Andrew has the apron doubled up and tied high under his armpits, so he won't trip on it. My grandmother can be heard making her way up the basement stairs, and Grandfather hotfoots it up to my bedroom to change out of his bathing trunks before she catches sight of him. She wouldn't have said anything to him, of course. She wouldn't have to.

I look at my grandmother where she stands at the head of the stairs with her hands on her hips. "Your father did a decent job on that wiring."

Andrew and I gawk at her. These are the most unlikely words to be spoken in our house. My father rewires when he's nervous, and he's been very nervous lately. It occurs to me that my grandmother, between teaching my father how to cook and to sew, might have given him practical home improvement lessons as well.

The food smells great and we all sit down together to a delicious meal cooked by Andrew. He's at the head of the table, spooning the soup into bowls, hacking at the chicken and passing out beautiful white, uneven slices. He stirs the gravy and spoons out beans and potatoes. It's the nicest meal we've had in a long time, and I go to bed with a new respect for my brother.

As usual, my dreams buck and roll under me. Sometimes, when you sleep, you are aware of everything: the fact that you are dreaming, the room around you, the strange logic of your own dreams. I can hear Andrew breathing the way little boys do when they are exhausted. I can sense my grandfather moving in the hallway, and yet I am horrified by the floor under my bed, which swells and breathes like a living thing. I know that, soon, I will fall off and see whatever this thing is, as clearly as an insect sees a shoe. But as the bed sinks away to nothing, I find that I am awake. Birds have appeared in the trees outside the window and a weak yellow sun filters through the curtains. I sit up and stare at my brother, who is small and pretty and restful.

For a long time I've had the strange idea that he and I were born the wrong way around. He should have been born first, born female and given to my grandmother, who always wanted a daughter but got boys instead. My brother should have been me. And I should have been born later, and male.

Of course, years later, when my brother grows huge and muscular and bearded and leaves home in a truck to go to college, that idea will seem absurd. But in the moment it strikes me as horribly true. My parents are gone, shot into orbit by something out of our control, and my grandparents roam through our lives in their own perplexing patterns. How would it be, that other life? I lie back and watch the sun come across the ceiling and I picture things as they might be, picture myself as a boy, and it's not exactly difficult. I don't tell myself that things might be better. I don't tell myself anything at all.

FISH-SITTING

.... MY BROTHER HAS STOPPED
talking. All he does now is read: kids' books, adult books,
newspapers, the cereal box, pill bottles, signs, advertise-
ments, and scrawls on the sidewalk. He's the best reader
in his class, but no one can make him talk. I'm looking at
him now, lying on his stomach on the living room rug.

"What're you reading, Andrew?" I say. But he just holds
up *Asterix*.

I go back to spying on the new neighbours with the
binoculars. The new neighbour lady, Mrs. Draper, is out
drinking on the grass of her backyard with someone who
isn't her husband. In this way, she is just like the previous
neighbour lady. My mother says that maybe it's something
about the house itself, maybe there's a gas that comes out
of the basement and makes people crazy. She's convinced

Mrs. Draper is having an affair with this man, and it looks like she's right. Mrs. Draper has her foot up on the man's thigh and she lets her head fall back, sun beaming on her exposed neck. He's rubbing Mrs. Draper's ankle and touching her leg. He's got his back turned to me, but I can see red hair under his baseball cap, and on his forearm. He leans over and retrieves a bottle from under her chair. With Mr. Draper the way he is, I'm not surprised Mrs. Draper has opted for this.

I can also see my father across the street, talking to the Bison. I named our neighbour "the Bison" because he's got a huge head with woolly hair that starts too far back. I imagine a sci-fi world where everybody looks like that. The Bison is kind of shuffling around on his front mat, the blare of sunset throwing his lumpy shadow across the front door. My dad's at it again. I can tell by his expression: open, fatherly. The Bison is spilling his guts.

When Dad comes in, I say, "What did he tell you?" Andrew glances up at Dad, wiggles his nose to adjust his glasses.

"The Bison? Oh, well, he's worried about selling junk bonds, and he should be, because it's just a disgusting thing to do. He's attracted to Mrs. Shiffler down at the corner, and…um, I think that's all. Oh yeah, his first sexual encounter was with his cousin."

That's my father these days. He's spending more time talking to people outside the family, mostly because he can't talk to Mum, and as time goes by, he's getting better at it. People seem to trust him, to want to confide in him; he's the stranger on a train. They take one look at him and decide it would be much better to get that niggling little secret out in the open. Men confess to impotence, cheating on their taxes, a desire to drive into oncoming traffic. One lady confessed to poisoning her husband's dog because he always kissed it on the lips. "It was repulsive," she said.

It's a relief to find out how really warped other people are, because our own home life is a mess. My parents have decided to separate and my mother is moving out soon. We are all floating now because, even though the change has come, nothing has happened yet. Meanwhile, I'm not doing too well in school. I don't know what it was, but I felt I was suddenly on holiday and I had nowhere to go and nothing important to do. My dad has been taking me aside and doing his best to scare the shit out of me about what happens when you let yourself go, but I still feel like school is something other people have to care about, not me. I sit in class and enjoy the sound of talking, but I'm not really there. Some of my teachers worry about me. I see their mouths move, but it never occurs to me to wonder what they are saying. And then at night I stay up late and stare through neighbours' windows using my binoculars.

Sometimes, walking along the street, I pass by a face I've been spying on and it's hard not to say hello. Or worse, to say something like: "How's the zit cream working?" or "Why do you let that cat lick your toes?" It's true, there is a lady who puts her feet up on her coffee table so her cat can get up and lick her toes. I'd go through the roof.

. . . . . .

It's ten o'clock at night, and I see Mr. Draper coming up the drive to his house. He swaggers, fumbles with the key. In the dark he lets a bottle drop and it smashes on the stoop. Mrs. Draper has locked him out again. I watch as he disappears into the house, leaving the door ajar. In a minute, Mrs. Draper comes out with a dustpan and pokes the shards of glass onto it with a fingernail. Then she's gone and the door is still open, the hall light beaming through the door and glistening in the pool of booze outside.

I can tell something's going on downstairs in my own home, but the fight is pretty quiet as usual, no raised voices. My brother comes in and sits on my bed with a book; sometimes Andrew crawls under the bed and reads, with only his head and shoulders sticking out.

My school report is a wall of rejection, and what's worse is my dad can see that I don't care. My parents are talking to me about it and they are like wolves working as a team to pull something down. This is one of the rare moments when they co-operate. I have to admire their self-control. I know I'm a pain in the ass. I know I should be promising things, acknowledging faults, or at least trying to look worried. But I can't even manage that.

We're in the kitchen, with the back door open and a lawn mower droning away two lawns over. I am on auto-pilot as usual, watching my parents' mouths move, listening to the grinding machine as if it might tell me something useful. When I come back into focus, my father is sitting back, looking satisfied. My mother gives me a kiss on the forehead and then leaves the room. I realize that I've agreed to something, but I have no idea what it is. Two days later, Mum gives me a book from the library on tropical fish. "I thought this might help," she says.

"Thanks," I say. Apparently I've agreed to do something about fish.

I've always hated school, but now even my girlfriends there are acting as if I've got some illness they don't want to catch. We're sitting at a greasy spoon eating fries and gravy, drinking coffee.

"You know," Ginger says, "you used to be a lot more fun." I can tell she's angry for some reason, glaring at me, stabbing her fries in Rosalie's gravy. It's obvious they've been talking about this, because Rosalie looks panicked, like she's thinking maybe she'll go to the washroom right about now.

"You spend too much time with Marty. I don't know what you think is so great about Marty. She's not a normal person."

"What do you want me to say?" I ask, and it's a real question. But Ginger doesn't take it that way.

"See, Hazel? That's what I mean. You think it's everybody else's problem. You totally change, and it's everybody else that's screwed up, right?"

Rosalie jumps in to save me and tells Ginger to lighten up, what's the point in getting upset, and those are the last words I hear, because I tune out again. I know that if Rosalie wasn't here, Ginger would be pulling out the big guns and talking about my parents, maybe saying I'm unbalanced because of them, or maybe that it's my fault what's happening to them, and therefore to me. Everything she says is familiar, and it all translates into *You are getting on people's nerves.* I watch the cook scrape the grill with a spatula, the oil rolling up under it, the thin hiss of metal on metal.

· · · . · · ·

My mother comes into the living room and looks at me and Andrew. Andrew is reading the TV *Guide*, sequentially, as if it were a novel, and I'm spying on the Drapers.

Mr. Draper is home and I can see he's throwing sofa cush-ions around. I wonder why a man would come home early from work to do that. I stop and look up at my mum. She has another fish book.

"This is for when you fish-sit."

"Oh...yeah," I say. "When is that?"

"I can't remember, but I'll call her and ask." There is the sound of something smashing next door. Mum bends down and looks through the curtains. "Maybe I'll wait a while," she says.

I stare at my mother in disbelief. This is incredible.

"I have to fish-sit for the Drapers?!" I say. But she's look-ing at Andrew where he sits, his face four inches from Thursday night.

"What are you reading, dear?" she asks and strokes his hair. Without looking up, Andrew raises the TV *Guide*.

· · · . · ·

It's night. On top of being a zombie all day, I can't sleep properly either. I wake up every hour or so to seethe with frustration. I look through the binoculars but there is never anything to see anywhere. Why can't these people do something interesting? Aren't there neigh-bourhoods where people are up all night killing each other? Tonight, I decide to do something useful. I read about fish.

Fish are pitiful pets, really, but I can see why someone might want a tank in their house; some of them are
lovely. There are Japanese fighting fish with their long
tails and mutating colours. Glass catfish that are com-
pletely see-through. Mollies. Tetras. There are sharks the
size of a stick of gum. Hatchetfish with their fat bellies.
Piranhas with underslung jaws, which can grow to the
size of trash-can lids. I gaze at photos of iridescent scales
and emotionless eyes and small snapping mouths. I gaze,
half dreaming, at photos of dissected fish, the mushroom-
like frill of gills, the strange little sacs and organs all
balled up together. There is a plastic ruler, measuring the
wreckage; a white pointer, indicating nothing.

Andrew comes into my room and we sit together on my
bed with our backs against the wall, reading. Neither of us
turns a page for half an hour, but our eyes move, wandering over lines of print. Andrew still won't talk. My mother
kisses his hair; my father squats and whispers to him and
presses his forehead to Andrew's; nothing works.

· · · · · · ·

Tuesday, 9 a.m.: excellent. The most excellent things
about today are that my mother is calling the movers
and that I have the twelve-minute run at school. Ginger
claims she has her period, but the two phys-ed teachers
stand in the door to their office, not buying it. They're

both huge, spongy, and blond, and they wear stopwatches
that hang to their groins. One is a man, the other a
woman, and no one could ever see the difference between
them. Rosalie and I get dressed while Ginger begs for her
life. She's just going to have to hurry in the end and get
into her gym clothes like the rest of us. Marty comes in,
her jean vest looking even tighter than usual, and we all
stare at her as we change. She strips quickly, and a dozen
pairs of eyes gaze openly at her body, knowing she will
start last and finish first. With a body like that she could
walk through walls. Marty is my friend these days
because, as she puts it, I'm a freak like her.

Lilac bushes and mock orange float past over an
undulating field of nausea. I feel like I have needles in
my lungs. Every time I run into the sun I feel ten pounds
heavier, and every time I pass under a tree I feel human
again. When it's over I sit in the change room and sleep
with my eyes open. As people dress and leave, two
doors swing open, then swing closed, and a sliver of the
hallway can be seen. Marty is out there waiting for me,
smoking.

When I'm ready, we go for fries and gravy. We smoke
and eat at the same time, which grosses out the waiter.
As usual when I am with Marty, I chatter like an idiot
and she listens to me in amused silence. I make up weird
facts and theories about things, such as that curly hair

means your mother didn't get enough sleep; these are things that I know would bug Ginger. Marty almost never talks; she gives me room. Marty has failed school for two years already; she's older than any of my friends and she lives by herself in an apartment. Once in a while her twin brother, who looks nothing like her, pulls into town on his bike and she disappears for a week or two with him.

I grab Marty's cigarette and finish it while she fishes another out of the pack and lights it. No one has seen Marty for quite a while, and she's made no mention of her brother, which is intriguing. When I ask her where she's been lately, she grabs the butt out of my mouth, stubs it out.

"You're tired," she says. "Go home and sleep."

But I can't go to sleep. Today is the day I have to go over and meet the Drapers, get instructions about their stupid fish, and my mother has made me promise to thank them for the jam Mrs. Draper made.

I drag Andrew along for moral support and he follows me like a sleepwalker. When Mrs. Draper meets me at the door, her face jumps out at me, younger than I thought and more friendly too. I've stared at that face many times but never seen it up close. Andrew glares at Mrs. Draper through his glasses until she invites us in and takes us around the house to look at what she calls her "babies."

There are tanks everywhere, built into walls, standing in hallways, a big long one separating the living room from the dining room, and all of them have sheets of paper taped to the glass. On the papers are written instructions, the names of the species of fish, and pet names with quote marks around them. "Dingus." "Ralphy." "Slow Learner." In the fridge is a canister of brine shrimp and lettuce for the shark, Arnie, and a shallow dish of larvae for the rest of the fish. I look at the larvae lying inert beside the Parmesan cheese. I make a mental note to tell my mother to throw out Mrs. Draper's homemade jam.

Mr. Draper keeps his distance from me but I can smell booze on him from where I am, a stink like orange juice that has been left in the sun. Andrew, who Mrs. Draper tried in vain to butter up, is staring now at the lists of names and dates, the feeding and saline instructions, as if he's committing them to memory. I have to drag him by the elbow as we go from tank to tank. Every time I look at Mr. Draper, he looks over at his wife with a shallow, wary grin. She's leaning close to the bright blue tanks and gazing intently at the fish where they swim in slow, pointless patterns. Then she tries to show me a sick crab, which I can't find among all the greenery and pebbles and toy castles; everything I see turns out to be a rock. She tells me that if the crab dies while they are away, I shouldn't blame myself.

A car horn goes off in the driveway and Mr. Draper says, "Jeff." A furious look comes over Mrs. Draper's face and she hustles us out the door, making me promise to thank my parents for offering my services. Andrew doesn't need to be pushed and is already halfway back to our house. The Drapers wave goodbye to us and wave hello to Jeff. I recognize him; he has red hair, is not as thin as I'd thought, wears sandals, and he has a pair of mean blue eyes. I pause on our porch to see Mr. Draper give Jeff a long, affectionate bear hug and slap him on the back.

"I think that man is their son," I say to my mother. She's in the living room, tossing the cat in the air and saying "Yikes!" over and over. The cat is as limp as a doll and he's purring.

"What man?"

"The one you thought was having an affair with Mrs. Draper," I say.

"Shh!" She looks absurdly at the wall as if they might be able to hear us through it. "Really?"

"The husband gave him a big hug."

"Well, they could all three be...you know..."

· · · . · · ·

Marty is whistling into the empty school hallway. She says the only way to find out about the Drapers' visitor is to come right out and ask Mrs. Draper. This is typical of

Marty, who has the social graces of a snake. I can picture Mrs. Draper standing on her doorstep stunned, and then fainting. The only surefire way to find out is to sic my dad on the Drapers, but Dad has opinions about whom he will bother pumping for info, and he thinks the Drapers are creepy.

"Fish," he has said. "Fish is typical of that couple."

I'm thinking about that when Mr. Butcher comes down the hall and I elbow Marty. She lowers her arm, in which she has a cigarette. A No Smoking sign hangs in the cloud over our heads. Marty is taller than me, so Butcher doesn't see me until he is quite close. The look on his face changes then, from nervous to blank. "No smoking, ladies," he says as he passes us, and after a second Marty snorts two pencils of smoke from her nostrils.

· · · . · ·

By the time I'm in school the next morning I understand that I'm disappearing again, like a TV signal bizzing into a simple white dot. One minute I'm by the window in G44 with an untouched test in front of me and the sun is shining through and I can see my hands lit up on my lap. The next minute I am in a basement hallway, on my way to another class, looking at a pipe. Rosalie grabs my belt loop and drags me to art class. She got bored waiting as I stared at a pair of initials gouged in the drywall next to the pipe. I don't know whose initials they are. Just two people. Maybe it's all over between them, maybe they aren't even in school anymore. I tell Rosalie we should scratch a crazy date in there, 1902, and see if anyone notices. It's exactly the kind of anal little thing that annoys her about me. She shoves me into a chair, then crosses the room to get away from me. I watch the teacher's legs come out of her shorts and her elbows that never straighten.

. . . .

It's only the second night I have to feed the fish, and I'm already in the habit of leaving the lights off when I walk through the Drapers' house. I like the way the blue tanks light up everything and shadows of fish move like clouds over the walls and carpet. The tank lights are on timers and the water is heated, so all I have to do is check the temperature, use the saline meter to make sure the water is salty enough, and give the fish a tiny amount of food. Fish eat practically nothing. I open the wall units at the top, slide back the grill, and drop in a pinch of food. It's a foul-smelling kind of lumpy mess. Some of it floats on the surface and some of it drifts down through the water in clots. When I get up on the chair, the fish go wild and they dart at each other, stab right into the air at my fingers, and shoot from the top of the tank to the bottom, scattering the little blue stones. The crabs tuck in under their shells and the snails sucker themselves tight against the glass, as if a bomb was going off.

Arnie the shark stops moving when I come upstairs and into the hallway, his lidless eye looking at me sideways. He's only as big as my thumb, but I think of him as dangerous. The books say sharks refuse to mate in tanks; they'd rather chew each other up. Arnie drifts closer to the glass, staring out at my white T-shirt suspended in the gloomy hall. I drop a lettuce leaf in and he stabs and nips at it. The leaf flips and drifts in the lighted water like a sheet carried away on the wind.

Later, I sit with my feet up on the dining room table and watch the fish or spy through the front window with my binoculars. I have a whole different perspective on the neighbourhood from the Draper house — I can see clearly into different rooms. At about nine-thirty, the lady with the cat usually calls someone on the phone. She pulls her hair around and looks at the split ends up close. She points her finger at the air like she's giving an invisible person a lecture. My guess is that it's her sister on the phone. I bet there's a lot of fibbing going on, sentences that start with: "And I told him, I said: 'Look!...'"

Soon, the cat lady hangs up, eats out of a small tub of ice cream, and watches TV. Then her cat gets up on the coffee table and licks her toes. It hunches over, looking urgent. I can hardly stand it — I have to get up and scratch my scalp and walk around the room in the dark. I also learn that zit-cream boy shaves his armpits. Maybe he's a speed swimmer or something. Maybe not. Then there's a teenager I think is the Bison's daughter. She smokes, leaning out her window, and stubs the butts out on the shingles and lets them roll into the eavestrough. Downstairs I can see Mrs. Bison cutting things up: fish, carrots, sausages, frozen lasagna, hunks of grey meat. Mrs. Bison is good with a knife.

But it's all so dull, really. And so it occurs to me to look around inside the Drapers' house. They have a few sexy books on the shelf above the bed, books with creative suggestions, but they've kept these next to a medical dictionary with horror-show diagrams and photos. It's a combination guaranteed to put the idea of sex right out of your head. I look in drawers, open the bathroom cabinet and inspect bottles and clippers and foams. But it's a bleak search. No rubbers or sex devices. No drugs. No embarrassing poems or letters. No medications for anything gross or sad. I spend a long time and come up with nothing.

I make my way downstairs in the dark, Arnie whipping back and forth in a panic as I pass, and I grab my binoculars and head for the door. But something stops me. I don't really want to go home these days; I don't know what to expect when I come in the door — maybe one of my parents fuming silently, or talking to Andrew, trying to communicate with Mars. I stand in the Drapers' hall and look through the binoculars at our front door. The doorknob appears, big as a pumpkin, motionless and strange. I swing the binoculars round, trees dissolving, colours and shapes blurring and reforming into the outline of my father.

"Dad," I say.

He is standing in the backyard of our house, in the dark, with his hands in his pockets. He's just standing there, thinking. And suddenly I see my father for what he truly is: kind, confused, and moving day by day into a future he can no longer elude.

HIPPIES

·· I'M SITTING ON THE ROOF OF
my house with my legs hanging over the edge. I'm
squinting, taking turns putting one running shoe, then
the other, over the parked cars below. Four roofs over
there's an orange cat with a fat head regarding me bale-
fully. I've never seen him before. Maybe he lives up here,
eats birds out of the air. He swivels his big head and
looks down at the sidewalk, where someone is standing.

"Oh my God!" cries a voice.

It's Mrs. Baze. She's four foot something, wears funny
hats, and has badly crossed eyes, one of which she has
angled up in my direction. She moves her head around
to get me fixed with the other eye, then legs it up the
steps and into my house.

"Uh-oh," I say. "Mrs. Baze and her gaze." That's one of my mother's.

Our TV aerial creaks in the wind as I lie back and let the sun fall on me. The cat steps away over the gravel and soft tar.

Sometimes I come up here at night and look out over the city, at the twinkling lights and the cars going down the streets. Planes pass overhead, invisible except for the flashing lights, the tiny faraway hiss of engine. Looking up, I can feel the house sinking under me and the soft black sky spreading out like something alive.

The best thing is when people go down the alleyway and I can drop pebbles. They look at the ground for a while, cogs turning in their heads; finally, they look up. I have to laugh. I see people walking along below, swinging their arms. My father passes down the alleyway with the lawn mower, and he tells me to cut it out, without looking up, without stopping.

But Dad doesn't really care. And there's the porch roof one storey down, so why worry about me falling? But a kid on the roof is the worst thing for Mrs. Baze. I feed her idea that young people are wild. For example, she's convinced that hippies congregate in the park out back of her house and throw their empty bottles of hooch over her fence. It might have happened once, but in her mind, the debris is always flying—it's a neighbourhood emergency. The world worries Mrs. Baze: she sees trouble and inconvenience everywhere. She takes her worries to the police, the firemen, the hydro guys, door-to-door salesmen, her vet, any neighbour who stands still too long. I've seen her in the Safeway, bending over the bags of sugar, saying, "This *can't* be the price!" Boys in red aprons just stamp the goods and shuffle along the floor away from her; they keep stamping, keep shuffling.

· · · . · · ·

"Don't let her catch you again, or I'll kill you," my dad says. He and Andrew are scraping at pots that got burned during one of our disastrous dinners. We all cook together now that my mother is gone; it's a daily duty. This fact bugs my mother so much I have to make sure never to mention food in front of her.

"Why didn't he think of that when I was living there?" she said when she first found out.

Dad's unusually pissed off today; maybe it's the heat. He hacks at a snarl of rock-hard spaghetti.

"I had to go look at her birds to shut her up," he says. "You wouldn't believe the stink."

Mrs. Baze has a knack for being present when birds get swiped by cars. She takes them to the vet, sparing no expense to save the dwindling life. The vet begs and reasons with her, but it does no good. Once the vet kept an unconscious patient overnight for "observation," and then put it down in secret. But Mrs. Baze caught on to that. Now she follows him into the back room, watches his every move while the vet keeps up a vain monologue on "prolonging the inevitable."

"I'd change vets," she told my dad, "but this one gives me a discount."

Mrs. Baze has an old parrot that has been with her for ages, and two badly addled pigeons, Valentine and Bigs. None of them flies farther than sofa to chair; Bigs walks into walls.

· · · · · · ·

It's Tuesday. A stifling, humid day when the trees droop and the street seems to fade into nothing halfway down. Andrew sprays me with the hose and then I spray him. I hold the dog down in the mud while Andrew soaks his coat, and the dog groans under my weight, snapping irritably at the stream of water. Dad comes outside, so we go after him, and it doesn't go over well. He stomps inside to change his pants.

"Why's he wearing pants in this heat, anyway?" Andrew says. I try to hide my shock: Andrew's talking again. Just like that.

He and the dog follow Dad in, trailing water and mud and crushed grass behind them.

The tap drip-drips against the porch step. My head swims for a second. The back gate opens and I turn to look. Nobody's there, and then my mother is there, her bare feet sinking into the mud. She's looking down at the tracks she's making, the perfect marks of toes. Between two breaths, she's gone, leaving nothing, no sign.

· · · . · · ·

My friend Jeannie says she's miserable; she can't sleep in the heat any better than me. I've called her very late, and now she's reading me stuff as we both lie in our beds. I ask her about my horoscope, and she talks to me about past lives and birth control and her mother. Jeannie's Korean and she looks up our birthdays in her books. My sign keeps changing: year of the ox, year of the rat.

"This book is crap," she says, and I hear a clatter in the background as the book falls to her bedroom floor. We ignore the clicks and sighing as my father checks the line, checks the line.

· · · . · · ·

My dad stands in the bathroom scrutinizing his own sour expression in the mirror. He is wearing a tuxedo with the dust of years on it. Today is Castor and Netty's twenty-fifth wedding anniversary and my father will go, alone, out to the car and drive the fifteen miles to the

Silver Birch Golf Club, which Castor has booked for the evening.

While Dad's gone, Andrew and I filch a beer each. Andrew strikes one match after another until two packs are gone, then flushes them all down the toilet.

Dad comes home very late. He slumps at the dining room table with his tie dangling, taps his finger on the wood, scratches a little light spot. I bring him a beer and he thanks me, but doesn't touch it.

"How many people," he says, "can say they fit into a twenty-year-old tuxedo?" He holds out his arms in a weary gesture, totally without pride. Jeannie says my dad is a babe; so's my mum. Too bad about me. His clear blue eyes, his tanned hand tapping again at the table.

· · · · · · ·

"They're still just lying there," I say. I'm up on the roof, watching the couple across the street do nothing in their bedroom. Jeannie has come up with me, but she prefers to stay well back, close to the attic window.

"Okay," Jeannie's voice says, "did you know that in mythology the crow is symbolic of death during sex, you know, like old men who take young wives and have a heart attack?"

"Get out. Really?"

"Naw. But it sounds good, doesn't it?"

Help Me, Jacques Cousteau

Way to the east, you can see the light of a train passing along the uneven walls of warehouses. The sky is silky and black; it feels like there isn't a breath of air anywhere on earth. Jeannie shifts uncomfortably. She doesn't like heights. Also, I know she doesn't see much point in sitting up on a roof. She sighs and flicks a pebble at me.

"What are they doing *now*?"

. . . . . .

I'm trying to sleep, relaxing my toes, then my ankles. Fat lot of good it does. Two guys on our street are playing *Miami Vice*, cars squealing around corners in the middle of the night like dogs chasing each other in circles. I've moved my bed under the window so I can look up into the branches of the trees. I remember my feet dangling down from the roof. Headlights pan across my ceiling, attended by a screech of tires. The headlights make several passes and then, finally, don't come around anymore. It is quiet, dark. I gaze up into the tree, and for a moment I think I can hear the leaves chattering to themselves in aggrieved little voices.

In my dreams I venture forward into the dark, placing my feet carefully between sharp flagstones. A brutal light keeps blaring on and off — it is hard to see where to walk. I look down to see a crow in the gutter, caught under something wet and mossy, its sleek, muscled neck writhing in its attempts to pull free. I grab at the dark mass and discover that it is made of pine needles, resin, clay — a gluey weight that clings to the bird's body as if feeding there. I hear my mother's voice, sharp in my ear, saying: "*Nothing* is worth that." I wake up quickly, blindly identifying my body's angle across the bed, acknowledging the ambulance light that flashes in the air above me.

· · · . · · ·

It's morning and the dog is hopping up and whistling in his throat. Mrs. Baze's parrot sits in his cage on our fridge, angling his head and examining, with one disc-like eye, the questionable business below. We don't know the parrot's name yet. Valentine and Bigs have gone to another family, one without a cat or dog. Last night, the neighbours who gathered to help outside Mrs. Baze's house decided that our dog was gentle enough, and the parrot looked tough enough, and so we got him.

Mrs. Baze's heart medicine made her retain water. She kept fainting in her house, finally staggering out onto a neighbour's lawn, where she fell down, jabbering, in her nightie. She calls hourly from the hospital and asks us to put the phone up to Florio's cage for her to shout to him. The bird bites his toenails and opens his mouth to show his dry little stump of a tongue. Andrew puts a stick in the cage and Florio snaps it in half with one lightning-fast strike.

· · · . · · ·

"They took three bags out of me," Mrs. Baze says, pouring me another cup of grainy tea. "They put this tube up my —*you know*, and it stretched me out. I still have to wear pads." She sits down with a heartfelt sigh in her chair and looks out over her garden. I, too, take in the willow tree, the ivy-burdened fence. There are flowers growing in rows and clumps, bordering the lawn and hanging out of windows, petals staining the patio bricks. Some are lush and thick-stalked, others bent as if by fatigue. Still others peek from doorways like consumptives, pale, with shrivelled stalks and leaves chewed to shreds by cats.

"You sure have a green thumb, Mrs.—" I begin to say, just as a beer bottle comes whiffling over the ivy-covered fence and lands with a clink on the grass. It's my father's brand.

"There!" Mrs. Baze cries, triumphantly. She fixes me with that bizarre gaze.

"*You're* my witness!"

This is the moment Mrs. Baze has been waiting for. She is electrified, up out of her seat, shaking her little fists over the cookies and tea cups, shouting abuse at the air. The parrot stands on the apex of his cage, tethered by the ankle to the top ring, flapping his wings as if to mock her. I can't believe it — hippies really do throw bottles over her fence!

"Oh!" says Mrs. Baze, just as if someone had hit her, "Oh!" I reach out to hold down the rattling plates. I blow tufts of dry feathers away from my tea.

Somewhere beyond the flowers and ivy and leaning-over trees, behind the soft running footfalls of the retreating bottle-thrower, I hear my brother's low giggle.

BOOMERANG

me remember Mr. Whitnell. Her memory is perfect and she feels I am underprivileged because I can never remember anything. At least, I can't remember anything in its right order, and I rarely know if it's a real memory or just something I heard somewhere. If you have a mother like mine, your own memories become unnecessary.

I go to her house in the late afternoons sometimes, and she gives me a cup of her jitter-producing coffee. Lately, she's been working on my childhood memories, prodding me, bringing up traumas and excitements I only dimly recognize as having happened to me. It's my mother versus the fog in my head.

Today's subject is Mr. Whitnell, who used to live on our street and, as my mother puts it, used to go "screaming around at night." He lived six doors down from us in a small blue and green bungalow. He had some disease of old age, or perhaps the problem was latent in him all his life. One way or the other, there would be sounds of a disturbance in that house, things breaking, his sister shouting his name over and over like a parrot.

"And then, crash!" my mother says. "Out he runs, all over the street, howling. Are you telling me you don't remember this?"

I say I don't and my mother regards me silently for a moment.

"You're not so good on things previous to last week, are you?" she says.

I admit for the four hundredth time that I'm not. I remember last week in Technicolor, but that'll fade, soon enough. I do remember bits of my childhood, like hating every square second of elementary school, especially recess, when I was supposed to go out and have "fun" with people I didn't know. There were dogs and cats I felt closer to than most of the girls at school. I remember the seasons going by. I remember a dentist coming to do a talk. He had a huge plastic tooth and an even bigger red toothbrush and I remember him dropping the tooth on the floor by mistake.

"Well, look at that!" the dentist said, trying to cover up. "See how strong tooth enamel is?"

And I remember summer in my neighbourhood, the trees crowding over the sidewalks, maple keys sticking to my shoes, the sidewalk, the windshields of parked cars in the morning. Everyone seemed to have kids at the same time—they were all my age. After a while, people had more kids, and those were all the same age as my brother. I don't suppose it could really have been like that, but it seems that way in my mind.

· · · · · ·

My dad has a boomerang, a real one, and it sits up on the mantelpiece, leaning sideways, as if someone has come in from killing kangaroos and left it there. He used to make rough ones from plywood, and he'd teach any kid who wanted to know how to throw it. He'd go out to the park, kids holding on to his pants pockets and his hands, and he would whip the boomerang into the air and watch it swoop up. A moment later, my dad and eight kids would hit the deck as the boomerang snapped back over their heads. I only saw him catch it once, a single, beautiful moment when he reached up and it came back to him. Usually, he and his short entourage would have to fetch it from where it had embedded itself in the grass like a javelin.

Neighbours called on my father all the time. For broken lawn-mower blades, flooded garages, even bread recipes.

I remember an old lady begging my father to come over to her house. She was angry or frightened, it was hard to tell which. When I ask my mother about that time, she knows right away what it was.

"That's when Mr. Whitnell faked being dead. His sister fetched your father, pretending to be in a panic, but all she wanted was to embarrass the old man. He was there on the couch, holding his breath like a child. There, see? You do remember him," she says.

Again I have to say no. What I remember is the blue and green front door, half open, the windows with their gauzy curtains, and the few waxy tulips that drooped off the porch.

Next door to the Whitnells was a dog that howled and howled, as if a madness had come over it. The young couple in that house kept getting dogs for their little girl, and the dogs kept getting loose and disappearing. They called two of them by the same name because the girl got so upset about the first one getting away. The two dogs looked nothing alike, but perhaps the name was enough to calm her. My father sawed a big stake for that family and hammered it deep into their lawn and attached the dog to it by a long, thick rope. The man thanked him, and that dog never got away. Still, it seems no dog could lead a normal life in that house. The little girl soon ceased to give a shit about pets, and every day the dog would go round and round the stake, wnding up the rope, until his cheek touched it.

"I've been having dreams about your father," my mother tells me, "and in one of them, we're supposed to get married. The church is right there across the street, and your father is in his coveralls, those blue things, and he is wiping the ceiling. I ask him, 'Why aren't you dressed? They're all waiting for us!' and he looks down at me like I'm crazy."

She slaps the table and looks at me. "I should have known about that man."

I tell her it was just a dream, she shouldn't get so worked up. But I too have watched my father climb on tables, up ladders, onto two stacked chairs, wiping the ceiling before company comes over. He takes off his dress shoes, removes dishes and cutlery from the already set table, and fiddles with the overhead light or removes cobwebs. There's my dad, up on a chair, forehead beaded with sweat, turning as the doorbell rings. I tell my mother, however, that her dream was just a dream, not a message.

Dad's still living in our house and Mum has a place of her own. They're both different now, with fewer ups and downs. I occupy a difficult space between them. I go to school, hang out with my friends, and wonder which one of my parents will go off in me some day, like a time bomb. If I could choose, I don't know what my choice would be. Dad marches around after dinner, start-ing three projects at once, and then falls asleep on the couch having finished none of them. In the meantime, without ever seeming to sit down and do it, he's man-aged to carefully mark a pillow-sized stack of students' papers. He remembers every student he's ever had — the city is littered with them now — but he doesn't remember any of their names. He has trouble, sometimes, remem-bering mine, and he runs through the family names one by one till he gets to me.

My mother, on the other hand, has a trick: she says, "Give me a word, any word at all, and I can think of a song with that word in it." Sometimes she calls me at night and says, "I've got it! It's a little song about a hardware store, and in it is the word *grommet*." She remembers all the words and sings the whole song through.

When I was younger and my parents were still together, some older boys hung Mark Wilson up on a fence by his underwear. Mark was a little bastard, but those kids hurt and embarrassed him, and he hung there for a while before some of us found him. Most of his clothes were on the grass, far beneath his kicking feet. We weren't tall enough to reach him, so we ran to my house and got my dad. When my mum asked what was up, we pretended it was nothing. She stood there and watched us rush my father off to the park, dragging him by his fingers. Dad lifted Mark down and the boy immediately ran away, crying and holding his clothes against himself.

In many ways, I'm a morbid person, ready to think the worst of people. I wonder if a thing like that — like a boy's humiliation — stays with a person and changes them in subtle ways. I always read the front pages of the newspaper first, all the mayhem and blood. I skim through encyclopedias of murderers, and it seems that each one had a small trauma, or a strange childhood, or something in them that grew like a bad seed. I read these books at bedtime and then have dreams where I get shot, and my last thought is always, "Oh, shit!"

Mark Wilson is grown now and has gone to Thailand. My mother believes he went to join a cult, but my bet is he's a Buddhist. My father doesn't remember him, doesn't remember pulling a boy in his underwear off a fence. Dad's almost as bad as I am. I come reeling home from Mum's, drunk on my own history, and try it all out on him. But there's no way he can help. Say, for instance, that the neighbours down the street return a belt sander or an extension cord to him. Dad will hold it in his hand like an unexpected gift.

"Is this mine?" he says.

"Okay," my mother says to me, "remember when your best friend, what's-her-name, moved away and you spent a summer with nothing to do and I wanted to strangle you?"

I do remember this; I remember the girl's letters being perplexing, as if they'd been written by someone much younger. I remember being frustrated and bored and yelling at my mother, her face blooming with anger. Later I was sitting in the bath crying, a common event that summer, and the window was open, with the cool air coming in. I stood up and sobbed onto the window sill, splashing my feet. Just then, Mr. Whitnell shuffled by out on the sidewalk. He was in his slippers, with no pyjama top on. I watched his skinny body slide past, his scrawny chest raw as a plucked capon. He was hissing. I expected to see someone else running after him, but no one came. There were little smacking sounds, as if he was hitting a lamppost with a stick. Then Mr. Whitnell shuffled and hissed back the other way.

"I knew you'd remember him if you tried," my mother says. "Some time around then, he lost his voice and got much worse, so they took him away. Poor old thing, his sister just gave up on him. That's the way it is with relationships."

Mum is satisfied, but I still can't picture Mr. Whitnell's face. It's as if these are stories I heard and only imagined I was there. The whole thing disturbs me sometimes. I feel like an alien dropped into this family, while the real me, along with my memories, is somewhere else, lost.

· · · . · · ·

I go home from Mum's and sit with my dad, our feet up on the coffee table, watching TV until the test pattern with the Indian chief comes on. My dad has been asleep since he put his feet up, and I'm lying beside him like a zombie. I elbow him and say, "It's tomorrow already, Dad." He erupts from the couch, his sweater crooked, and staggers towards the stairs, his arms out in front in case he bumps something.

"Dad?" I say, as he creaks up to the second floor. "Do you remember Mr. Whitnell? That old man down the street?"

"Who...?" He rubs his face.

"Mr. Whitnell. Remember?"

"Oh God," he says. "He fed you so much candy once you puked all day. We never told your mother how that one happened." I want to ask him more but he's already gone, hustling upstairs to hog the bathroom. Tomorrow, I think, I'll ask him tomorrow, and I close my eyes. The test pattern is still glowing in the dark inside my head.

I imagine myself sitting on the back steps with Mr. Whitnell, and there is a bunch of chocolate bars lined up in front of us. He's saying: *Six plus three?* and I'm saying: *Eleven.* He's laughing and saying: *Try again, try separating them into two bunches. Six and three?* Before lunchtime we finish them all, even though Mr. Whitnell is diabetic, even though his sister is in the sunroom, snoring, perhaps dreaming of being free. I can see his face perfectly, and the trees beyond, and the crooked back fence. Mr. Whitnell is a cute old guy, with cloudy eyes. My dad appears at the door, and Mr. Whitnell and I look up to greet him, our faces and fingers sticky with chocolate. My dad gets all these different expressions on his face, one after the other, a string of veiled and unhappy thoughts.

I don't know what happens next. My neck hurts from sitting on the couch too long. I shift a bit, and soon I'm asleep. It's Utah this time, and I'm driving, and everything is truly bizarre.

THE ELECTRIC CURTAIN

························· I'M IN A DISGUSTING MOOD
this morning, sitting in a shaft of sunlight and thinking
about my ex-boyfriend Nick for the first time in a long
time. To keep busy, I look for the piece about my brother
in the newspaper, folding the pages out over my toast
and coffee, but I can't find the right section. It's a com-
munity newspaper, with print that stinks like cigars.

So far, everything in the paper is about our neighbourhood's pitiful blues festival — a disaster that goes
on for a week; you can listen all day and never hear a
single blues tune. Some days, you stand on your porch
and the sounds of the various bands drift together, playing "The Girl from Ipanema" and "Bad, Bad Leroy Brown."
The mess goes on all day and into the night, tunes coming
through the bedroom window, forcing me to cover my

head with a pillow. I wake up humming songs I hate. The newspaper chirps at me: "This Thursday!"

For some reason, I woke up this morning thinking Nick was going to buy our house. I struggled out of bed to warn Dad, and was halfway down the stairs before I realized it couldn't be true. I sat on the bottom step then, my head in my hands, and tried to convince myself that I wasn't on my way into another Nick fixation. Nonetheless, the carpet under my feet didn't seem to belong to me anymore. I was a bit worried; before this morning things had been going so well for months.

I finally find Andrew in the "Home on the Range" section of the paper. It's the kitchen section, but some weeks they run out of food tips and typo-riddled recipes, and they throw in anything that might have happened *near* a kitchen. Today, it's Andrew's solar-powered curtains.

"Look," I say, as Andrew digs around under the sink, "it's about your curtains."

"Huh," says Andrew.

"They call you a genius — actually they call you a *gerius* — and it says that solar energy —"

"Those curtains don't work. They're crap," he says. This is his opinion of almost everything he does, and I've given up telling him not to be so down on himself. I'm looking at a grainy picture of my brother's face. He is intent, serious, holding up a little solar chip.

"You look like a grown man here, Andrew," I say, holding the paper out.

"I *am* a grown man," he says.

It's true; he's seventeen years old now, six foot two with arms like a boxer's. If he keeps growing at this rate, he'll soon be able to pick Dad up and bounce him on his knee.

My brother yanks a long string of nylon rope out from under the sink and inspects the frayed ends. He exits the room, leaving the cupboard door open and dragging the rope behind him. The dog stares at the twitching frayed tail as it rounds the corner, but he doesn't rise to chase it.

In many ways, my brother is an updated version of my father. Between the two of them, they have booby-trapped the whole house. Everywhere there are devices that have been strung up, tied together, rigged with electrical tape and timers and light-emitting diodes and beepers. Apart from the curtains, which I know are Andrew's, I'm not sure which project belongs to whom, and anyway, they collaborate. My father has a coffee maker on his bedside table that turns on when his alarm goes off. The problem is that, if he turns the alarm off, the coffee stops brewing. Every morning, my father leaps up and heads for the bathroom while his clock *raaangs* away under a pillow.

The doorbell plays Christmas music, the garbage bin is booby-trapped against the dog as well as raccoons, and

Dad's car gets really good mileage. My father is in heaven, having finally convinced somebody that a life without gadgets is no life at all. Even my mother has softened and allowed Andrew to do a few things around her house, though she keeps asking for the doorbell's tune to be changed to something other than "Silent Night."

During the day I work for an optometrist who calls me "sweetie" and very obviously loathes her job. At night I come home, drink beer, and write my ridiculous poems. Occasionally, I write something that makes sense, but mostly the poems are about lizards and apes and the A-bomb, which is why I'll never get famous. I can't seem to write about normal things, like, say, the optometrist and her fancy shoes and the crying sessions I hear from inside her little darkened room. She thinks I can't hear her. But I can practically hear spiders walking, and now I know all about my boss, about her fondness for white powder, and her less than happy relationship with Revenue Canada.

In fact, it was during one of her crying jags that I met Nick. If I were more like my mother, I would have considered that, in itself, to be a bad sign. I came out of the office door at a near-run with mail under my arm, hoping my boss would be finished weeping by the time I got back. I passed a workman who was repairing the marble by the elevator doors. He was bent over, so all I saw was his long back, and his butt. Later, coming back the other way, I smiled broadly at him, and he swivelled on his heel to watch me go.

Over the week we began taking time to visit with each other. I'd stand with him, leaving the office door open so I could get to the phone quickly, or else he'd sit on his toolbox beside my desk and drink coffee. On his last day, I asked him out to dinner. He looked as if the question had caught him off guard, and he stammered a series of little nothings. For a moment I thought I'd made an error in judgement—he didn't like me; he didn't like girls; he was gay. But then Nick stammered that he'd like very much to go out, and he shoved his hands in his pockets, leaned forward, and kissed me on the cheek.

The next night we were sitting in a little restaurant so cramped they had to hang the bread basket on a rope over the table. Almost right away he told me he had a girlfriend, and he was feeling guilty. I stared at him.

"Why did you come, then?" I said.

He said because he'd wanted to, but he was confused. By then, we were both confused, and neither of us could eat anything. I picked at my food and so did he. We sat there trying to smile or talk. After a long, depressing interval, we paid and left the restaurant.

In the municipal parking lot where he had parked was a gang of little boys, and they chased each other like puppies and struck at tires and bumpers with their sticks. Nick was going home, and I was going home, and I knew he wouldn't offer me a ride.

"Well, thanks," I said.

He leaned over and kissed me on the cheek again. I should have turned and walked away, but I stood there like a fool, waiting. Then he started kissing me again, in earnest this time, pressing his groin and thighs hard against me. It was great. After a little time, we became aware of kissing noises from the shadows, and so we hurried away down darkened streets to a place by the water. We stood stupidly staring at a warehouse. The wind blew on my face and I closed my eyes against the airborne grit. Nick said he thought he should be going.

We had this superb fight about why we were there together and who had started it. By the time we left each other — both furious and dazed — Nick had unbuttoned my shirt, pulled my skirt up, I'd had both hands down his pants, and we'd shouted at each other twice about who was being manipulative. It was amazing.

Of course, Nick called me at work a week later. We saw each other secretly, irregularly. The sex was honest, but not unusual. At work, I'd whisper into the phone to him while patients dozed in the waiting room. This went on until he felt compelled to tell his girlfriend. Then it was all over — for two weeks.

I was sitting reading on the back porch when the phone rang, and it was Nick on the other end. I went straight over to his apartment and had sex, the kind of sex that, in retrospect, gives you a little shock that it actually happened to you. In the kitchen afterwards, he kept glancing nervously at the clock on the stove, and I figured it was time for me to go.

I confessed to Andrew about all this; I tell him about most things, and he followed the story attentively. But when it was over, he shook his head.

"What happened to the guy with the beard?" he asked. "I liked that one." I looked at him, unable to remember who he was talking about.

The weeks droned on and I didn't hear from Nick again. My friend Jeannie told me, "You should be proud of yourself for surviving him." But she also said, "If you ever find yourself being cheated on, you'll know you deserve it." In private moments, I found myself rehearsing confrontations with Nick until, over the months, my accusations became mantras, then the words meant nothing, then I forgot he existed.

· · ·. · · ·

Sitting in the optometrist's silent office, with its rack of ugly frames and its files and order forms and past-due bills, I gaze at the closed door and listen to the elevators as they hum up and down. A patient, late for her appointment, crashes through the door, knocking over the coffee table and a half-dead plant.

"Made it!" she barks, her lenses fogging into blind discs, and just then I hear a tremulous sigh from the examination room behind me, and the snap of the lights being turned on.

It's official now: I want another job.

When I get home, my grandparents' Cadillac is parked half in the driveway, half on the lawn, and steam is coming out of the bathroom window upstairs. The keys are still in the ignition, but the car is empty. Andrew is in the garage leaning over his motorcycle and a girl is standing next to him, smoking. She asks him what he's doing *now*, and he tells her to put out the cigarette.

I've seen the girl annoying Andrew before; she's the daughter of the Bison, the ugly man across the street, and everyone agrees that it's lucky she doesn't look like him. She's about fifteen and pretty, a hint of a widow's peak on her forehead, a mouth like a poppy. One evening, she even stuck around so long we had to ask her to have dinner with us. She and my father had a great time discussing her parents' peculiar marriage. For instance, the Bison tells his wife when he's on the verge of having an affair and begs her to go and talk the other woman out of it. My father found this quite demented, if entertaining. During all of this, Andrew looked at me as if it was my job to get rid of the girl.

I go inside the house and stand in the hall listening. Someone is having a bath, and I conclude it's my grandfather. I scrutinize the calendar, but there is nothing there to indicate that Dad is expecting his parents to visit. My grandmother comes rushing out of the front room, thrilled.

"The curtains are electric!" she says to me as she passes.

"What are you doing here, Granny?" I ask, but she's gone upstairs to tell her husband about the boy's latest invention.

My grandparents don't remember names. I think that's why they gave their sons such odd names: Castor, Bishop, and North, names that don't exactly blend in. I have been called "Becky," "Annabel," even "Tony," whatever comes to mind. My brother, generally, is "the boy."

My grandfather comes down the stairs in a towel, trailed by my grandmother. He ignores me and goes into the front room, where he stands brazen in the window and puts his hand over the solar chip. The curtains, thinking it's nighttime, slowly draw closed.

"There!" my grandmother crows. "You see?"

He takes his hand away and the curtains squeak open again. He does this a few more times until the mechanism makes a low hum and finally seizes, halfway closed. We scatter, hoping Andrew has seen nothing.

I've got music on the radio in my room and I'm lying on the floor, smoking a cigarette. My boss and I started smoking around the same time and, for some reason, we still hide it from each other. "Want some coffee, sweetie?" she will say, already halfway out the office door.

"No, no!" I'll cry. "Let me get it." But she's out the door and I sit back, glaring at her retreating lab coat. She gets to smoke and I don't, and we both know she owes me one.

I watch the smoke curl towards my bedroom ceiling. The music stops and an ad for the blues festival comes on, an awful *oom-pa-pa* in the background. I sit up, infuriated: *oom-pa-pa*!? Why call it a blues festival at all? A woman's voice purrs that there are only two days to go, admission is free, and then she names a bunch of bands with stupid names. Jim Dandy. Fred Moodie and the Mississauga Mood Mix. My favourite is a couple of idiot guys called the Two Tones. I whack the clock radio off, put my cigarette out, and stomp downstairs.

I find Andrew at the dining room table wiping the grease from his hands with a yellow cloth. Grandfather is still swishing around in the bath, humming. I figure he said something mean to my grandmother again, because she has taken off in the car, leaving a long streak of burnt rubber on the street outside. I can picture my grandfather up there, reading a magazine, unperturbed.

"How's it going?" I ask Andrew.

"I should have bought the Honda. This machine wastes oil."

I'm so irritable, I feel like I might cry. "Andrew," I begin, but my voice drops off and I don't really know what I was going to say anyway. My brother glances at me, his face alert. He's a good-looking young man, and I can see why the girl pursues him. He's not stupid, either, because he stands, comes around the table, and hugs me and thumps my back. After a while, he sits back down and takes up the oily cloth again.

"Andrew, why don't you like that girl? She's pretty, isn't she?"

"Yes, she is."

"She likes you, right?"

"She likes me, but she's fifteen years old."

"So what? You're only seventeen."

"Fifteen is young; that girl hasn't even got all her teeth yet. That's a fact. You get your last teeth when you're twenty-one."

I'm considering my brother, and Nick, and I'm wondering: do I have some kind of problem seeing the impossible for what it is? There was this time in high school I went on a diet because I wanted Maria's brother to notice me. I wouldn't eat Christmas dinner, sat with a plate of dry toast in front of me, until my mother couldn't stand it anymore and asked me to leave the table. I went down a waist size, got a lot of colds, and it was all for nothing. To Maria's brother, I was just another little girl, all of us squealing away up in Maria's room, no better than a box of puppies.

Sex isn't the problem. I don't seem to have any trouble with sex, and most of my boyfriends are nice people — the guy with the beard, the law student, the petty criminal, the wine expert, the guy with the truck. I liked them all fine. But once in a while, I pick some guy and lose my mind over him. Maybe it's the poetry; maybe it's got some kind of side effect.

Dad comes through the door, dropping his briefcase, bags of groceries, and a new leash for the dog, because the last leash got buried.

"What happened to Andrew's curtains?" he asks. From above, there is the unmistakable sound of someone's backside squeaking around in the tub. Dad looks at Andrew, looks at me, looks at the ceiling, and then curses, swearing his way into the kitchen.

· · · . · · ·

It is a cool, damp night and the dog hops around in the dark backyard, woofing at a squirrel. The squirrel tightrope-walks along a telephone line, past the upstairs windows, and then disappears into the blackness of a tree. Sitting outside on a garden chair, I listen to the sounds of rotten blues bands warming up several blocks over. By the end of a week of this music, I will feel like I've been scrubbed endlessly with a bristle-brush. Tonight, I make a bet with myself that the first tune I hear will be something from *Cats*. To my surprise, the sounds form themselves into a giddy, tumbling version of "Trouble in Mind." I stand up, intrigued, and walk out the back gate to see what's going on. My dad and Andrew have escaped already, and my grandparents are asleep in front of the TV, where a lady cook chatters soundlessly.

People stream along the sidewalk, often forced onto the road. Streetcars inch carefully through the crowd, empty and inviting. Most restaurants have a band glittering in the front window under temporary lights. Some bands are arranged on the sidewalk, while several battle each other in the park, electrical cords running everywhere and light stands wavering in the crowd. I know from experience that, later in the evening, there will be a few drunken scuffles, people swinging punches at empty air, cars burning rubber up and down the streets. I am looking for my father or my brother, but instead, under a woozy string of lanterns, I see Nick.

I think: *Great, perfect, fucking hell*, but I still find myself walking towards him through the crowd. He sees me coming and turns to escape. A woman next to him grabs at his shirt, the way one grabs at a child who runs too much, but she misses him, shrugs, goes on talking to her friends.

I follow Nick around the corner and down a side street, dark from the overhang of trees. Cars line the curb and people's fences lean out over the sidewalk. It is quiet here, and the air is damp. I am running on a high, staring at Nick's perfect, fascinating, panicked face.

"Don't you ever think about me?" I say, advancing on him.

"This isn't good—"

"Answer me."

Nick gawps at me, mouth unhinged. I get closer, and he doesn't bother backing away. He seems to be calculating something.

"Do you ever think about me?" I say, softer.

"Yes," he admits, reddening.

"What do you think about?"

"You know, just…"

He's cornered, squirming in the shadows, and I am about to have a heart attack, my pulse out of control. We both stand there, stunned and waiting.

"Remember the time in the truck?" I say. "Do you remember what you said?"

He aims a furtive look over my shoulder at the light coming from the street.

"I miss you sometimes," he murmurs.

"There! You see?"

"What?"

"You're so maddening. I can make you admit things that aren't true."

"Look, I don't know—"

"I bet I can make you want me again."

"I'm leaving now," he announces, but he doesn't move.

"Sure, go ahead. You'll go home tonight and you won't tell your girlfriend anything about this. And you'll wish you'd taken the chance to kiss me again—no one's looking, no one would know. You'll sit there over breakfast and wish you had."

He grabs me then, on cue, and kisses me. We both look back at the street and then shuffle into the shadow of a parked van where we can do it some more, pulling vainly at shirts and belts. The sound of people's voices comes to us from the distance, a small warning, moving closer, then drifting away again.

Nick stands back to rub his face. "Can we just wait a second, here," he says, indicating his pants, adjusting himself cautiously. "I have to wait."

He leans on the van and watches me while I fix my clothes. His is a remote, disturbing gaze, and I know, with certainty, that I can look forward to another couple of months of mental illness. A car goes by and Nick seems to awaken as the lights sweep his face.

"I have to go," he says.

"And I just have to do this one thing before you do," I reply, and I slap him hard. It's done before I know what I'm doing. He gives me a simple, mean look, but he seems almost pleased. I watch him walk away, back to the light and noise, his hands stuffed into his pockets, his cheek burning.

By the time I get home, all the lights are off, except for the oven light, which glows yellow as I retrieve a beer from the fridge and a frozen cigarette from the icebox. I see the next few months spread out before me like a cold, dark sea, and there's nothing I can do about it. I just have to wait for everything to return to normal again.

Our dog pads in and slumps heavily on my feet, forcing me to yank them free. I have no idea why he does this. He came to us after my mother left. Perhaps it was my state of mind then, but I never expected him to stay. He still has a collar around his neck that says he belongs to someone else, someone who moved or at least changed their telephone number. We haven't even named him, just call him Dog, and it doesn't seem to matter to him.

Sometimes I worry about running into Dog's real owner while I'm walking him. It's a scene I often imagine in detail: a man hurrying across the street, calling out, the dog pulling on the leash, barking. There will be a warm reunion, followed by an awkward moment, the dog confused, wagging, the dog belonging, for an instant, to no one. Then, the real owner will smile, his hand extended to take the leash. I see myself giving the dog back; I imagine the man thanking me.

Sometimes, thinking about this, I panic in the middle of a walk and turn back home, hustling Dog past the smells that clamour for his attention — trees, fences, garbage cans, the hubcaps of cars. I feel that the only thing keeping him with me is the leash. But Dog shows no real sign of leaving. The front door of our house is usually open all day, and, when I feel uneasy, I go and watch him sleep in a patch of shade on the driveway, not moving, the sun falling down, and nothing changed.

THE FUNERAL

life where, without thinking, I strike like a cobra. The hotel kitchen boy doesn't speak English — standing there, red-faced, by the open back door, a cigarette dangling from his hand — but he knows what I'm suggesting. Christmas Eve is tomorrow and I can smell the food being prepared. I haven't figured out where exactly we're going to do what I'm proposing, and before I can, I spot my dad and realize it's time to duck down a hallway, perhaps come back later to work things out.

There are lances hanging from the walls and dark red tapestries, and beneath them are chairs too stiff to be sat on. Also hung on the halls are paintings of horses that look like overripe fruit, great huge rumps, tiny little hooves. The walls are stone, the floors are stone too, with carpets running everywhere, and there's stained glass in the lobby.

"This is crazy," my mother had said when she arrived, but she sounded thrilled, looking around at the "insane luxury." Bishop said the place reminded him of horror movies. We stood around, our luggage at our feet, taking in the tourists who came and went, the mounted heads of game animals, the chandelier, the runner carpets snaking away into dark hallways. Castor seemed happy; we were all together.

We're at a hotel in the mountains where every guest seems to speak a different language. We've taken four adjoining rooms in the old wing: my father and brother together; Castor and Netty; Mum and me; and Bishop with his most recent woman, the overweight Auntie Merry. My grandparents can't come because they're not talking to each other again.

The trip was my uncle Castor's idea. He owns the hotel, or part-owns it. No one really knows where Castor gets his money or what he does with it. Whatever the case, the staff know who he is. They murmur to him in various languages, he's allowed to make his way through the staff hallways, and he gets memos and his mail brought to him. It was his idea to invite my mother, who arrived with a small yellow bag, took one look at my father—whom she clearly hadn't expected to see—turned back to Castor, and said a word I'd never heard her use before. My father looked stricken. Castor threw his hands down in disgust and wondered why he had even bothered.

We were all together for the first Christmas since anyone can remember, and right away we heard that someone in the hotel had died. So we'll be going to the funeral in town. My dad heard about it first, of course, but he's not clear on who died.

"Typical of this family," my mother says. "We're going to a funeral, but we don't know whose."

The hotel is jammed with people. I watch a woman wearing the largest fur I have ever seen drift close to the bellboy, and kick him as she passes. From the bellboy's dull glare, I suspect she does this a lot. My father is roaming the lobby, talking to people and finding out as much as he can. He speaks passable German and French. He finds out what people do for a living, how much they make, and why they've come to the hotel. I spot him by the huge front doors, working on a fat man from some place where they like suede a lot.

"Any idea who died?" I ask my uncle Bishop. He's sitting on the pool table reading a European royalty magazine. His face says he's never seen anything so disgusting.

"Parasites," he blusters. "Breeding and sleeping in late and sipping brandy." He picks up an amber-coloured drink next to him on the pool table's felt.

"Look at this so-called man," he says. "Look at the state of him. His head must weigh fifty pounds." He marches off in disgust to show my father. As soon as he's gone, I guzzle what's left of his drink.

· · · , · · ·

I've managed to convince the kitchen boy to come up to my room. I have him on the bed and I am lying on him. He's laughing and trying to unbutton his white uniform. I jump up and pull the heavy curtains closed and the room is sunk in darkness. When I go back to the bed I have to be careful not to knee or elbow him. I'm hoping my mother, who shares my room, doesn't come in. But she's downstairs in the lounge with the rest of the family. That's where I was too, until I spotted the kitchen boy wandering down the hall with his paper crown.

Later, the kitchen boy, whose name is Hans, shows me a back stairway the staff uses. On the door to the stairs there is a big sign in four languages saying an alarm will sound if opened, but Hans pushes the door open anyway and shows me where the wires have been grounded on an overhead pipe. We sit in the stairwell and he teaches me the German words for all kinds of body parts, and before too long, I begin to wish he'd go away. My mind drifts off to a young man I saw earlier, standing by the concierge, looking lost.

· · · . · · ·

"Dad—" I start, dodging people coming in the front door. "Dad, do I have to go to this funeral? I might not feel well. Maybe it would be better if I stay in my room, read a book…"

My father is looking over my head. "Hmm?" he says, giving me the bag of wrapped presents he's carrying. I watch him wander off to sit with my mother. To a stranger, my parents would look like any married couple. Their looks are similar; they have the same lilt to their voice, the same upright way of sitting. By now, even their handwriting looks similar. But my mother smiles at my father in a polite way, a smile she reserves for strangers. I feel myself floating a little, sick, as if the air has become gas, and I turn and flee to the other end of the enormous lobby.

I find Andrew standing at a wide bank of windows, looking out at the mountains, which glow red-hot along the peaks from the last of the sun. I hand him the bag of presents and he takes it willingly, holds it like a briefcase.

"You know what?" he says, "A woman just went by and kicked me." People stream past us, murmuring in German or Italian, men wheeling luggage dollies, children in their best winter clothes.

"It was on purpose, too," he says. I tell Andrew that I think the woman especially likes kicking young men. Andrew is gangly and tall, his hands and elbows grown wide, his face solemn, thoughtful. He nudges me and points out the woman in the crowd. She's a sight: a strange, over-stuffed creature in a grey fur, wandering amongst the party dresses and overcoats and steamer trunks and huge potted trees. We observe her as she navigates the lobby, passing by several skiers, a desk clerk—all young men. She does nothing to them. We follow her progress until she disappears down one of the low, dark hallways. Andrew looks at me in dismay, the bag of gifts dangling.

"What did I do?"

· · · , · · ·

There's a phone call in the middle of the night. My grandparents are fighting— in Nevada.

Bishop and my dad hand the phone back and forth like a hot potato and hiss at each other:

"No way, I do this too often!"

"Well, don't look at me!"

"Take the damn phone!"

"I need a drink," Castor says, looking on. We're standing in the hallway outside my father's room in our pyjamas, everyone's hair in a wild mess and pillow marks on our faces. Poor Merry is trying her best to melt into a corner; her pyjamas are like kitchen curtains, frilly and see-through. I can tell Andrew is in shock at the sight.

Bishop is speaking to my grandmother, holding the phone in a death-grip.

"No, don't! Mother, don't put him on!... Hello, Father."

"I need a drink!" Castor says.

"Of course you are, Father. No, just because you're seventy doesn't mean you're dead, however... you... *how* much?"

"Oh God!" says Castor.

"...in *two hours*?"

"It must be those bastards again," Castor says.

"Nooo!" my mother trills with enjoyment. "Not the famous Moe and Joe?"

"Who's Moe and Joe?" Andrew asks.

"Don't," Dad says to Mum. "Don't you laugh." She turns away and fiddles with the belt of her housecoat, her shoulders jiggling.

Bishop is squirming now. I can hear my grandfather's tiny voice from the receiver. He's telling Bishop that he loves him, and Bishop is wincing, swearing silently. I strain to hear the small, thin sounds coming from the receiver, try to picture my grandparents in a desert casino: the lights and mirrors, the spill of change overflowing cups and pouring to the floor, and outside, the cars cruising past the splendid marquees, their tops folded down, rolling through soft desert air.

Castor gives up on finding a drink, and snatches the phone away from Bishop. "Father, listen to me! Just tell them no and go get your—What?...I know you love Mother."

"Who are Moe and Joe?" Merry whispers.

"And I love you too, Father."

"Jesus!" says Bishop. By now, I'm wide awake. I badly want to get on the phone with my grandfather, maybe get him to tell me he loves me too. I wonder what it would feel like.

Castor puts his hand over the receiver and hisses, "They've got his car. Again!"

Dad flops down on the unmade bed, his hands between his knees.

"Oh, sure," Bishop mutters, "he tells *you* about the car, but does he mention it to me?"

Finally, Netty strides across the carpet and takes the phone.

"Gerald?" she says. "This is Netty speaking." Her voice is like a silk handkerchief floating down through the air. "Gerald," she says, "do try to concentrate."

When it's over, my grandfather has agreed that he's an ass. Netty holds some kind of power over him. She's single-handedly trussed him up in an invisible strait-jacket, made him promise to go home quietly. After that,

Dad and his brothers go in search of a bottle, and the rest of us file back to our rooms.

I lie awake and gaze at my mother — she's smiling even in her sleep — and I try to picture Dad and Mum together among the twinkling lights, rolling some dice. I puzzle for a while over whether it's hot in Nevada. With my father and his maps and charts, I probably should know, but I don't. After a while the image of my parents erodes and I see, instead, my father alone in Vegas, with his pockets inside out. I roll over, then turn my mind to other things, such as: if the hotel we're in has ghosts; if the ghosts are angry; if they died while in love or if they died in pain; or if they too had wanted to gamble and no one would let them. I wonder what kind of ghost my grandfather will make, because it's obvious he'll be one for sure. Then I wonder what kind of ghost I might be.

· · · . · · ·

The next morning, Christmas Eve, my mother comes into our room, puts a cup of coffee on my dresser, and sits down on the bed with me.

"How long have you been up?" I ask, grabbing the coffee.

"Funeral day," she says, not answering. "Thanks to your father." I'm ready to defend my father, like a fool, but Netty is standing in the doorway with Auntie Merry.

Merry looks haggard, trapped here with all of us. She tugs at her sleeves and pats her shirt down. Netty casts her eye over me, takes in the tie-dyed T-shirt I use as a nightie.

"Did your father buy you that?" she asks.

I pull the sheets up. "No," I say, insulted, "I bought it with my own money."

"Oh good," says Netty. "I thought maybe he'd lost his mind."

All the women, me included, take the elevator down to the lobby. My brother is there, sitting behind a computer at the front desk. His hair is still unbrushed, standing up like flames. The two clerks watch as I approach.

"Their root directory is screwed," Andrew says, and one of the clerks beams and pats Andrew on the back, enthuses in Italian.

No one knows where Andrew gets it, but he can walk up to any machine and fix it. He has never been seen reading a computer magazine, and yet he knows what's current, what's defunct, he knows machine languages. He puts a finger on a squiggle in a senseless wall of squiggles and says: "That should be one backslash, not two." The same holds true for more primitive machines: toasters, furnaces, cars. He bends over the oily mass of pipes and hoses in my father's car, grimaces, points at an unidentifiable steel lump. "You bought it used?"

After breakfast we find out more about the funeral we're attending. We've all been asking around, but without success. It seems that asking "Who died?"—especially when language is a barrier—can have unexpected results. Castor was told it was an entire family who perished in a fire, down in the city, nearly a year ago. Which clearly made no sense, as they'd already have done a funeral by now. Auntie Merry assumed it was one of us who had died, someone she hadn't met yet. Bishop thought he'd met a father with a missing child, so maybe the child was presumed dead... but it turned out the man was just showing him snapshots of a perfectly alive grandchild.

My father was able to sort it out, and now he explains it in detail while my mother squirms and sighs and stares at me as if I am responsible. In fact, the man who died was named Otto, and he was the organist at the church directly across from the hotel. He was eighty-seven years old, had dozens of children with several different women, and ate dinner and drank every night of his adult life in the hotel. He was a fixture, a local character, and now he is dead, and everyone in the hotel is invited to his funeral.

In the afternoon, Andrew and I descend the hill, following the road into town, our cheeks numb and our fingers screaming in our pockets because we made the mistake of whipping snowballs at tour buses and parked cars until the cold got to us. I like it when my brother lets me hang around with him, but still, I'm distracted, thinking about the phone call last night, and feeling sorry for old men who can't do what they want anymore.

"Do you think Granddad is crazy?" I ask Andrew.

"Yes," he says.

"How can you be sure?" I ask. I've been troubled by the suspicion that I'll end up like my grandfather — gambling, scaring the crap out of strangers, telling ridiculous stories so many times that I start believing them myself. For instance, I'm afraid to get my driver's licence. My grandfather was law-abiding at first, and then, one day, he parked right on the sidewalk, a boulevard of broken saplings behind him. It's been that way ever since.

"Oh, he's crazy all right," says Andrew, warming to the subject, "but Granddad was probably normal once, like you or me."

"Oh, no."

"I blame old age, I blame TV. You know, before TV, people had much higher IQs?"

"But what if —"

"It's true. Some dogs have the same IQ as a four-year-old human. Depending on the breed. And scientists think that some brain diseases come from too much..."

I'm so horrified, I tune him out. If it happened to Grandfather, it might happen to me. My worst fear would come true; I might not be me, after all. I might be someone else, someone really unpleasant, just waiting to pop open and spray all over the place, like a bad can of pop. I'll be old and crazy and never get a date. I'll be paranoid. Broke. Write abusive letters to the Queen. I'll never leave my house, squint through the drapes when the mailman steps on my porch. I'll stand over a boiling pot of water and hear messages about all the bad things Danny Kaye is saying about me. It's horrible. I look over at Andrew for help and only then realize that he's been trying to get my attention.

"*Look,*" he says, and takes my head in his hands and turns it, and I see the white rump of a deer walking lazily into the darkness of the trees. Its white tail flashes, blends in, and disappears. We walk on into town.

· · · . · · ·

The new clerk behind the desk in the lobby is smiling at guests with his nice white teeth. It's a dull, businesslike smile, and when he drops it he looks nasty, devious, interesting. He's twice my age, but I sit down on a plush sofa and consider him anyway. He's probably married. I am drowning in my own family, have no privacy, no room to manoeuvre. I have an overwhelming urge to go over to the desk and be frank with that man, watch his face fall, watch those white teeth stop smiling. Maybe he'd turn me down. Maybe he wouldn't.

Instead, I pace around the halls.

I enter a dim hallway, stare up at the beards of moose, the strange plastic noses of deer, their tongues stuck out a little, as if bleating. I am deep into a fit of the creeps when I remember Andrew's words about dogs being as smart as children. How smart are deer? I look at a mounted head and decide: not smart enough. What a horrible way to end up: wood and sawdust inside your skin, holding plastic nose and eyes in place. A woman ambles past, humming. People are milling about the lobby, huge animal heads lolling over them, and no one minds. Just me.

· · · . · · ·

An enormous number of hotel guests are crammed into the church as the funeral is about to begin. The minister comes in, to rousing organ music and children's babbling and the sound of dogs howling everywhere outside.

Andrew leans over. "If the organist is dead, then who's playing the organ?"

During the funeral service, my father sits at one end of the pew and my mother sits at the other. The rest of the family is wedged between them. Trying not to doze, I watch a man's smooth leather toe rise and fall gently in the quiet cavern of the church, as if the man is hearing music in his head. I fight the horrible wooze of sleepiness while the rector delivers the eulogy.

Otto, he says, was a good, kind, decent person, a man who gave such love to his children that he was wealthy in his soul as a result. He was generous to his friends, and generous to the world, since he gave the gift of music. My mother sniffles and takes my hand. There are a few quotes from the Bible about music and God's breath. I can smell Christmas dinner cooking across the street at the hotel. Dogs whine and scratch at the closed chapel door.

Two very old men are seated in front of my mother and me. One leans over and tells the other in a hoarse stage whisper, "We must be at the wrong funeral."

"Should have worn earplugs," hisses the other.

The rector, who is new, never met Otto, the man he is eulogizing. By the end of the service, the pews are boiling with unrest. This was Otto, finally falling dead in the pine grove, reeking of liquor, eighty-seven years old and halfway home. Otto, who threw things, who harried local girls and terrorized his many children, who badgered money out of people and never paid it back. Otto, tossing a cigarette down a bartender's blouse. Otto, drinking in church, the floor around his organist's bench foul with phlegm. Otto, called "the nickel man" by children in town.

At the reception afterwards, we all huddle like cattle in case someone should ask us what we are doing there, or in what way we knew the deceased. One by one we check our watches while the aroma of turkey and beef and steaming vegetables vexes and distracts us.

"Well," says Merry finally, in a tiny voice, "I don't think Otto would mind if we had dinner now, do you?"

We have all discovered, to our secret pleasure, that Merry is a glutton. She is furious and impatient, trying now to ignite the plum pudding with her plastic lighter, but it just won't start. She had wanted to give up and eat it unlit, but was vetoed. Netty keeps pouring rum over the pudding, so that by now it's sitting in a puddle half an inch deep. My mother is sitting beside me with her napkin at the ready in case anyone singes their eyebrows off. As usual when Castor is around, the noise in the room is almost unbearable. It's lucky we've got a little room to ourselves.

A beautiful waiter wanders around behind our chairs, making helpful suggestions to Merry, tripping on wrapped presents, and generally being a distraction. He has the outrageous name of Felton, he speaks English, and he has no idea how to kiss. His breath, I have discovered, tastes like cherries. I am gazing at his long face in the wavering glow of candles and the dim overhead light. He winks at me and my mother catches him; Felton turns red, grasps a few empty glasses, and rushes from the room.

"His name is Felton," I tell my mother, and she fixes me with an appraising look.

She's starting to catch on about me.

I take another drink of wine, sigh, wonder when we are going to open presents. For the last few minutes my father has been kicking me lightly, trying to find a comfortable position in which to sleep, and it looks like he's found one. I am always stunned at the way my father sleeps. Castor is laughing derisively at Bishop.

"What a crock!" he bellows. "I suppose you believe in the Loch Ness monster."

"Look, it's absolutely true!" Bishop is grinning.

"...and UFOs and ghosts. I suppose you pray, too. Does he pray, Merry?"

"Oh, you swine," says Bishop. Merry looks up from the alcoholic lump before her, lighter still hissing in her hand.

"What's so funny about praying?" She's saying it as much to Bishop as to Castor.

"Ignore him, dear," Netty says. "He's running his mouth."

We must be the worst guests in the hotel, which is probably why we have our own little room to eat in. Still, I'm feeling all right about the world. I've had more wine than I'm used to and everything seems gracious and happy and secure for once. I look at my mother, whom I miss a lot sometimes, and at Andrew, whose body seems to change every week, and for a moment I wish we could all stay like this. I think: wouldn't it be nice if we all died suddenly, without hurting, without knowing anything had happened, and went on as ghosts, having dinner and arguing and never growing old? What would be wrong with that? I wonder about my grandparents, old and wild as they are, without the first thought in their minds about mortality. And I wonder if Otto is anywhere around here, drifting through the halls, pissed off, invisible, throwing things at tourists.

I'm thinking about that, thinking about all of us, and the afterlife, and how maybe I could take the waiter with us, when, without any particular reason or warning, the pudding bangs on like a blowtorch. Blue flames leap at the light fixture overhead; chairs are shoved back in alarm, barking against the floor; Merry and Castor both scream.

One minute the room is noisy, the next, it's thunderous. Poor Andrew wakes with a jolt, blithering and confused.

"Substitute real oranges," he says.

The flames streak upward, and the air is filled with the aroma of hot butter, currants, and failing fireproof ceiling tiles. It's an emergency: my mother, with her napkin held up in absurd defence; Castor with both hands pressed to his mouth, roaring through his fingers; my father rising unwilling from sleep, smacking his lips, one serene eye open and unfocused on the blaze. It's fantastic, brilliant. I know then, this is the moment I've been waiting for: this is us, a picture of us, my whole family caught mid-sentence, mid-gesture, light pouring out, bright as a flash.

AUTHOR'S NOTE

I wish to thank the publishers of the original book, Tim
and Elke Inkster of The Porcupine's Quill, for their integ-
rity and goodwill; I also wish to thank John Metcalf for
his editorial honesty, and for speaking to me like a writer.
This new edition has been slightly revised to fit house
style and to address the occasional awkwardness. Many
thanks to Lynn Henry for bringing an older text up to
speed. And thanks, too, to Sarah MacLachlan. Without
them, this title would be out of print.

PHOTO: KRISTA ELLIS

GIL ADAMSON is the author of the bestselling and
critically acclaimed novel *The Outlander* (2007),
which won the Amazon.ca/Books in Canada First
Novel Award and the Dashiell Hammett Award,
was a finalist for the Commonwealth Writers'
Prize, and was a *Globe and Mail* "Top 100" selec-
tion as well as a *Washington Post* "Top 10" pick.
Adamson is also the author of two collections of
poetry, *Primitive* and *Ashland*. She lives with fel-
low writer Kevin Connolly in Toronto, Canada.